TRAVELED AND UNRAVELED

A DELIGHTFULLY DYSFUNCTIONAL FAMILIAL VACATION

THE DELIGHTFULLY DYSFUNCTIONAL SERIES

BOOK #3

A NOVEL

TIFFANY RYAN

This book is dedicated to my husband, Blake.
Think of it as a points accumulating event.

CHAPTER ONE

"I wanted to die," said Mom, yanking the cork out of the bottle of cabernet sitting on the counter. "I mean, I literally wanted to find a hole, crawl into it, and die."

"Oh, come on honey, it couldn't have been that bad," said Dad biting into his sandwich.

"Oh, believe me, Greg, it was." She poured the wine into a tall, stemmed glass and greedily imbibed, "In fact, it was so bad that I think we're going to need to find a different doctor for Beau because I never plan on showing my face in that establishment again."

"Don't be ridiculous, Olivia, I'm sure they're used to dealing with this sort of thing all the time," scoffed Dad.

"Oh, really?" she crossed her arms in front of her. "So you're telling me that it's common practice to rate your oral surgeon a one-star review on Google just minutes before being taken back to be anesthetized."

"Wait, what?" asked Dad, looking perplexed as he placed his half-eaten sandwich back on his plate.

"Yes, this morning I was not only tasked with the unenviable job of quieting your daughter's incessant and uncontrollable wailing, which by the way, is a story in and of itself, but I was also made privy, by the very doctor performing the procedure, mind you, that she had happily made her way onto Google just minutes prior to being called back for surgery heeding a warning to all that Cherokee Oral & Maxillofacial Surgical is both unscrupulous and a shameless poacher of time."

"Okay, first of all, the nurse said that crying is very normal when waking up from anesthesia, especially with girls," I groggily interjected. "And secondly, I was anything but happy when I left that review."

Mom and I had just returned home from being held captive at the oral surgeon's office for almost four hours, and while I was currently laid up on the couch icing my face and mourning my recently extracted teeth, Mom was filling Dad in on the highlights of our vexatious and distressing morning.

"I don't understand, how did they even come to find out that she had rated them a one-star in the first place?" asked Dad befuddled.

Mom took a generous sip of wine before answering, "I asked that same question, and apparently, the front office receives an immediate alert anytime a new review comes in, so once they realized that it had actually been written by a patient currently sitting in their waiting area, they immediately apprised Dr. Rosenthal of the situation, and he, in turn, decided to make me aware of it as well." She looked over at me irritably, "I mean honestly, Addie, did it not ever occur to you to post anonymously, or at the very least, use a pseudonym?"

"We waited three hours in that waiting room, Mom," I reminded her. "I was starving, nervous, and completely incensed by their ineptitude, so no, I wanted them to know exactly who it was coming from."

"Honey, they had three unexpected emergencies they needed to take care of first," answered Mom. "What were they supposed to do?"

"They were supposed to communicate that little tidbit of information to the eighteen of us sitting in the waiting room all morning," I growled. I shifted the ice packs, careful not to apply too much pressure to either side of my face, "And the only reason we even found out anything about the delay was because Dr. Rosenthal was freaking out about the review and apologizing profusely, hoping that I would change it."

"He was not freaking out about the review; he was simply apprising us of the situation." Mom reached into her purse and pulled out a small white pill bottle, "In fact, he was actually quite gracious and good-natured about the whole thing, so you may want to think about recanting some of what you said in that review."

"Your mother's right," said Dad. "Although I completely understand why you did what you did, I don't necessarily agree with the way you went about it."

Mom walked over, handed me four Tylenol and a glass of water, "Here take these, it should help with the pain." She lovingly stroked the hair away from my face and kissed my forehead, "Please promise me that the next time we find ourselves in a situation like that you'll refrain from insulting the persons in charge of your health and safety until after we've left the building; you're not your grandmother, you know."

"Who's not me, dear?" asked Grandma Helen, breezily making her way through the back door. She waltzed into the living room and immediately stopped short upon seeing my disheveled appearance, "Oh darling, what happened to you, you look simply dreadful."

"Thanks, Grandma," I grimaced.

"She's just had her wisdom teeth removed," said mom. "We discussed it yesterday, remember?"

"We did?" asked Grandma Helen confusedly.

"Yes, Mom, we did," she said. "In fact, we were sitting right over there drinking coffee when I told you." Mom walked back into the kitchen to retrieve her wine, "I believe I was finally able to make mention of it after the summation of your horrid dinner with Joan and before your lengthy disquisition on the wasteful prodigality of fondue."

"Well, you know how much I hate fondue, Olivia," sneered Grandma Helen. "It's always so tedious and labor intensive."

"I thought you liked Joan," said Dad, finishing off his sandwich.

I do like Joan, dear, I just detest her fondness for eccentric and overrated restaurants, that's all," she said flippantly. She walked into the kitchen and poured herself a glass of wine, "Quite honestly I think she does it to spite me."

"I hate to tell you this, Mom, but Joan isn't doing anything to spite you," said Mom, rolling her eyes.

"The woman chose fondu over Italian, Olivia, that is the very definition of spite!" She turned toward Dad, "I simply cannot for the life of me understand the allure of cooking your own food in a restaurant and then paying an obscene amount of money to do it, it's counterproductive and completely inane if you ask me."

"Honestly, I think it's more about the novelty of it all, rather than anything else," he shrugged.

"I wasn't aware that skewering meat and sticking it in a bowl of hot grease was considered novel," she retorted. "Apparently, I'm out of the loop on that one."

"Well no need to worry about that, Helen," said Dad, washing off his plate and placing it in the dishwasher, "We'll be more than happy to fix you right up with your own personal fondue set so that you'll be able to practice regularly and become proficient in the art of Swiss Bourguignonne cooking."

She glanced over at Dad, arching her brow, "I'd sooner kill you and have my grandchildren help bury the body before ever bringing one of those things into my home, Gregory."

"Aww, I love you too, Helen," he winked.

Just then Beau came downstairs with a tattered-looking paperback in his hands. "Hey Mom, I just finished that book on Julius Caesar you wanted me to read, and I must say, I actually found myself really enjoying it."

Mom set down her wine glass and walked over to him, "Beau, that book is over 200 pages, how in the world were you able to finish it in one day?"

"Wait, you were expecting me to read this whole thing?" He opened the book and riffled through the pages, "The entire first chapter revolves around Caesar's violent death, so how much more do I need to know? The guy's dead, end of story."

She looked at him as if he'd completely lost his mind, "Son, that's only the beginning of the story," she said. "There's so much more to learn about Julius Caesar's life than the fact that he was brutally assassinated." She pointed back toward the stairs, "No, you need to go back upstairs and read at least a few more chapters before you're done for the day."

"What?" he exclaimed. "I thought this was going to be a short read since he died within the first few pages."

"You can't possibly be serious," said Mom.

"He was a Roman, his wife had a bad dream, some depraved rich people stabbed him, and he died, what more is there to know?" he asked.

"What an eloquent retelling of history, dear," said Grandma Helen. "It's nice to see that your home education is working so well for you."

Mom glanced irritably over at Grandma Helen before returning her attention back to Beau. "I thought you said you were enjoying it."

"Yeah, I was, back when I thought it was only four pages long," he retorted sourly.

"You know, son, having a good understanding of Julius Caesar, and Ancient Rome in general, may come in handy during our time in Italy, especially with all the historical sites we plan on visiting," said Dad. He walked over and draped an arm around his shoulder, "In fact, you can be our personal docent when we go and visit The Temple of Caesar."

Last Christmas, Grandma Helen and Grandpa Anthony surprised the entire family with the generous gift of an all-expenses-paid vacation to Italy. The plan is to fly into Milan and then spend the next fifteen days traversing the beautiful Italian landscape starting in Lake Como and then making our way down to Tuscany, Rome, and finally, the Amalfi Coast. A few surprise events have also been orchestrated that neither one is willing to tell us about, so the entire family has been brimming with excitement and literally counting down the days until we leave.

"What in the world is a docent?" asked Beau.

"Someone who acts as a guide and informant to those visiting museums, but in your case, it means teaching the rest of the family all that you've learned about Julius Caesar while on location," smiled Dad.

"Ugh, fine," said Beau, defeatedly. "Can I at least get a snack before trudging back upstairs to read about this dead dictator guy?"

"I don't know, Beau, can you?" asked Mom, arching her brow. "I mean, you do have the capability of walking into the kitchen to get a snack, yes, but if you're asking whether or not it's alright for you to go into the kitchen to retrieve said snack, well, then that's something else entirely, now isn't it?"

"I see you're still in teacher mode, mother, so allow me to rephrase the question," he snarked. "May I please enter into our kitchen and retrieve a bit of nourishment prior to returning to my studies?"

"Yes, of course, you may," she said with a self-satisfied grin.

Before making his way into the kitchen, he briefly glanced over at me lying on the couch and said, "Looking a little rough there, Addie, are you sure they only took your teeth?"

"Shut up, Beau!" I snapped. "Mom, please get him out of here."

"Beau, that's enough," said Mom. "Your sister isn't feeling well, so just get your snack and finish up with school, please."

"Geez, I'm only pointing out the obvious," he shrugged. "It's not like the rest of the family can't see how bad she looks."

"You are such a cretin!" I spat.

"Well, at least I don't look like I'm storing nuts for the winter," he combated. "Tell me, Addie, which one is it that you're trying to channel, Alvin, Simon, or Theodore?"

"Alright, that's enough!" interjected Dad. "I have to get back to work and I really don't need to listen to the two of you maul each other in the background while I do it, so please, just go back to your respective corners and chill, alright?"

"Yes, sir," we answered solemnly.

Mom quickly followed Beau into the kitchen and gently pulled him aside, "You know, soon it's going to be your turn laying on that couch with ice packs on your face, and I highly doubt that you're going to want your sister treating you the way you're treating her right now, so let's take it down a notch with the teasing, okay?"

"Are you kidding, I think it'll be hilarious!" he guffawed. "I'm pretty dang funny now but imagine how funny I'll be waking up from a drug-induced state, I mean, there's no telling what'll come out of my mouth!" He grabbed a small bag of trail mix and a bottle of water before heading back upstairs, "By the way, I meant to tell you earlier that I was thinking about having mini corn dogs for dinner tonight unless, you know, you're already planning on cooking something and eating it is unavoidable."

"I'm making sausage and peppers," answered Mom nonplussed.

"Yeah, I think I'll just stick with the corn dogs, but thanks anyway!" he called out, running up the stairs.

"That child is incorrigible," said Mom, finishing the last of her wine.

"You know, I can't say I blame the boy, dear," said Grandma Helen. "Sausage and peppers are more peasant food than anything else."

"And you would know this, how, exactly?" asked Mom. "Last I heard, you grew up in a five-bedroom brownstone in the suburbs of Cleveland, not a cruck house out in the hinterlands of 12th century England."

Grandma Helen casually sipped the last of her wine with a smug expression, "You know, dear, I have yet to transfer that plane ticket over to you, so you may want to rethink that mocking sarcasm of yours." Mom reached for the bottle of cabernet sitting on the counter, emptied its contents equally into both glasses, and respectfully lifted hers in salutation, "Touché, dear mother."

Grandma Helen, mirroring the gesture, lifted her glass and smiled, "Salute, my darling."

Just then Aunt Christine came barreling through the back door, "Oh my God, you are not going to believe who just called me." She immediately stopped short, focusing her attention on Mom and Grandma Helen's full wine glasses, "And for the love of all that is holy, please tell me we have more wine."

CHAPTER TWO

Mom quickly reached into the cabinet and retrieved another bottle of wine, "Well, don't keep us in suspense, who called you?"

"Guess," smirked Aunt Christine wickedly, taking a seat next to Grandma Helen.

"I play this game enough with Beau, Christine, please do not make me play it with you too," sighed Mom, opening the bottle.

"Okay, I'll give you a hint," she smiled wryly. "The last time we saw him he was wearing a navy-blue Armani suit and looking like a guppy gasping for air as he listened to the judge award me an eight-million-dollar settlement agreement."

"No!" blurted Mom.

"Yes!" exclaimed Aunt Christine.

"Please tell me you're not talking about that philandering, good-for-nothing, ignoble ex-husband of yours," sneered Grandma Helen.

"That would be the one, yes," nodded Aunt Christine, gratefully accepting a glass of cabernet from Mom.

"Ugh, I absolutely abhor that man," she sneered.

"I think it's safe to say that everyone does," agreed Mom.

Grandma Helen slid her glass over to Mom, indicating the need for a refill, "He is a deplorable and worthless human being, Christine, and I will never forgive him for the hell he put you through."

"It's okay, Mom," she smiled, giving her hand a gentle squeeze. "I'm much happier now than I ever was back then, so truth be told, I'm actually glad he did what he did."

Eight years ago, Aunt Christine had the misfortune of learning firsthand that her husband, Jack, and best friend, Kaitlyn, were having an extramarital affair. As a freelance travel photographer, Aunt Christine often finds herself on location for weeks at a time shooting multiple campaigns for various hotel and resort chains around the world, so when she found herself finishing a Caribbean photo shoot earlier than expected, she decided to hop on the next flight home, pick up a bottle of Dom Perignon, dinner from their favorite Peruvian restaurant, and surprise Jack in their Lower Manhattan apartment. She barely had enough time to light the candles when he came bursting through the front door, lips and limbs passionately entwined with Kaitlyn's. The two were so enraptured with each other that neither one of them even noticed Aunt Christine standing there until she not so subtly cleared her throat, alerting them to her presence. Appalled and repulsed by the adulterous spectacle playing out before her, she immediately attuned herself of the situation, grabbed her coat and the unopened bottle of champagne, and walked right out the door, but not before pausing briefly to knee the two-timing scoundrel hard in the groin. Jack, of course, tried to downplay the situation claiming that it had only been a one-time thing, but the truth eventually came out that he had actually been having multiple affairs with numerous women throughout the entirety of their marriage. Believing wholeheartedly in the aphorism, "Once a cheater, always a cheater," Aunt Christine immediately filed for divorce and never looked back. Last year, while visiting the family for Grandma Helen's birthday, she was reunited with her old high school crush, Brian Caldwell, and the two instantly became inseparable. This past Christmas, Brian surprised everyone when he unexpectedly proposed to Aunt Christine. So, as soon as we return home from Italy, wedding plans and preparations are scheduled to begin.

Grandma Helen smiled faintly, "You know, it's funny, I still find myself daydreaming about that son of a bitch being waterboarded, bathed in gasoline, and set on fire."

"Mother, that's barbaric!" exclaimed Aunt Christine.

"No, scaphism is barbaric, dear," she sniffed haughtily. "What I'm talking about is much less messy and a lot more mainstream."

"What in the world is scaphism?" asked Aunt Christine.

"It's an Ancient Persian torture technique that is incredibly brutal and…" Mom stopped abruptly and looked curiously over at Grandma Helen, "Wait a minute, how do you even know what scaphism is, Mother?"

"I could ask you the same question, dear," she deflected.

"You know what, never mind, it's probably best I don't know," said Mom. She looked back over at Aunt Christine, "What I do want to know, however, is why Jack is even calling you in the first place."

Aunt Christine absently toyed with the stem of her glass and sighed, "Apparently, he wanted to congratulate me on my recent engagement and see how the move to Georgia was going."

"Mmm hmm, I bet," drawled Grandma Helen doubtfully. "And tell me, dear, how exactly was he even made privy to these new developments in your life?"

Aunt Christine rolled her eyes and slowly shook her head, "I may have divorced Jack, Mother, but I didn't divorce our mutual friends." She took a sip of wine, "Besides, it's not like I was trying to keep it a secret from him or anything."

"Well, that's unfortunate," sighed Grandma Helen. "I rather wished you'd had."

"What exactly do you think is going to happen, Mother?" asked Aunt Christine. "We've been divorced for over seven years."

"I don't know, but I definitely think he's up to something," said Grandma Helen. "You would do well to stay on guard and keep vigilant, darling, because he may very well be trying to slither his way back into your life."

"Geez, Mom, it's not like he's devising some sinister plan to break up the wedding and win Chrissy back," snickered Mom. "He was probably just calling to get confirmation on what he'd been hearing from everyone, that's all."

"That man is a self-indulgent, self-serving, bastard, Olivia, and I don't believe for one minute that his intentions are anything but sinister," she shot back.

"Okay, well, on a lighter note," continued Aunt Christine cheerfully, trying to sidestep the growing tension in the room, "Jack has graciously offered to reach out to a few of his restauranteur friends in Florence and Positano to see about setting up some dinner reservations for all of us while we're there."

"You told him about Italy?" shrieked Grandma Helen. "Why would you do that?"

"Why wouldn't I?" asked Aunt Christine. "It's not like he's planning on sabotaging our family vacation, Mother, he's simply offering to make dinner reservations."

"Well, I wouldn't put it past him," she grumbled irritably. "He's such an ass."

Aunt Christine looked over her shoulder and saw me lying on the couch, "So, how's our patient doing?"

"Well, now that she's calmed down and has stepped away from ruining legitimate businesses on Google, I'd say she's doing just fine," said Mom.

"I'm not sure what any of that even means, but it sounds like a good story," laughed Aunt Christine.

"It's a long story that I will happily fill you in on later, but for now, I should probably go check in on the patient in question." Mom set down her wine glass and walked over to me, "Hey, baby, remember to move your jaws up and down like the doctor said, it'll help with the healing." She took the melting ice packs out of my hands and gently stroked my hair, "In fact, you may even want to think about eating that peanut butter and jelly sandwich they recommended now that the numbness has worn off."

"I cannot believe they're actually expecting me to eat regular food after everything they've put me through," I growled. "Sadie said that she got to eat yogurt and ice cream for three days after her wisdom teeth were removed, yet I'm expected to eat a three-course meal an hour after extraction. I'm sorry but having me eat a sandwich just seems like cruel and unusual punishment."

"Dr. Rosenthal said that eating real food will help with the healing process and prevent dry sockets," said Mom. "So, instead of standing here listening to you complain, I'm going to put these back in the freezer and make you that PB&J."

"I'm pretty sure he just said that to torture me," I rolled my eyes.

"Well, maybe you should have thought about that before leaving that horrible review," she retorted sourly. She walked back toward the kitchen and then paused briefly, "Oh, and now that you seem to be a bit more lucid and a little less truculent, I'd like you to go back in and change it."

"Ugh, fine," I conceded.

Aunt Christine watched as Mom placed the ice packs back in the freezer, "Well, it certainly sounds like the two of you had an interesting morning at the oral surgeon's office."

"Oh, you have no idea," said Mom grabbing the bread out of the pantry. "It was definitely one for the record books."

Grandma Helen dolefully sipped at her wine, "You know, Christine, I really think it would be in your best interest to tell that philandering, miscreant, ex-husband of yours to crawl back under whatever rock he scurried out from and just leave you alone; he is not to be trusted, and you, more than anyone else, should know that."

"I know you're worried about me, Mom, but I need you to understand that I am truly the happiest I've ever been in my life," she smiled. "I am very much in love with Brian and have every intention of marrying him and becoming his wife." She gently took hold of her hand, "But I also need you to understand that Jack was a very big part of my life for many years. We were friends long before we were ever married, and if I'm being completely honest, I'd have to say that I somewhat miss the friendship I once had with him." Grandma Helen opened her mouth to protest, but Aunt Christine cut her off, "And before you say anything else, please know that I have absolutely no intention of letting my guard down or letting him affect my relationship with Brian in any way, shape, or form. I'm simply hoping to test the waters of friendship to see if we can't mend a few of the fences that were torn down after our marriage disintegrated."

"Well, I really think they were more obliterated than anything else, dear," snarked Grandma Helen.

"I'm a big girl, Mom, I know what I'm doing," she postulated.

"Yes, of course, you are, darling," smiled Grandma Helen.

Aunt Christine took a deep breath, "Okay, well, as much as I'd like to stay and chat, Brian and I are meeting his parents for a late lunch, so I really need to go and freshen up a bit, but when I get back," she smiled wickedly, "I fully expect to hear all about the day's events, and if there's video, I'll be wanting to see that too."

"Oh, believe me, I've got plenty of video," laughed Mom.

"You know, I'd really appreciate it if you would refrain from showing that to people, Mother!" I called out.

"Oh, calm down, Addie, I'm only kidding," said Mom. She lowered her voice and winked, "No, I'm not."

Aunt Christine stood to leave and then bent down to hug Grandma Helen, "I love you, Mom, thanks for looking out for me."

"Of course, dear," she said. "I love you too."

Grandma Helen watched guardedly as Aunt Christine walked out of the kitchen and up the back stairs, "That girl is a gullible twit," she hissed.

"That's a bit harsh, don't you think?' asked Mom.

"No, I don't, actually" she countered. She picked up her wine glass, rinsed it out, and set it in the sink, "Believe me, Olivia, that man is up to something, and it's going to be up to you and me to stay vigilant and make sure she doesn't do anything stupid or fall for his mendacious charm again."

"You know, Mom, we still have a few more days before we have to leave for Italy, so maybe you and I should just fly up to New York, do a little scouting, or maybe a stakeout or two, and then plant listening devices under his tables, bookshelves and lamp shades." She opened the loaf of bread, took out two slices, and put them on a plate, "Ooh, I know, we can even dress in black, harness ourselves from the ceiling, and then drop down into his living room just like they did in *Mission Impossible*."

"Are you enjoying having fun at my expense, darling?" asked Grandma Helen.

"Not particularly, no," said Mom, slathering peanut butter on a piece of bread. "I just think you're letting your imagination get the best of you again, that's all."

"I am not!" she said indignantly. "That man is egocentric, narcissistic, and completely devoid of all human emotion." She crossed her arms defiantly, "Trust me, he is definitely up to something and I have every intention of finding out what it is."

"Yeah, well, you also thought Mrs. Kramer down the street was a Soviet spy working for the Russian Intelligence Service, so maybe we should just cool it with the assumptions, okay?" said Mom.

"The woman was taking shots of room temperature vodka and chasing it with salted herring and boiled potatoes, Olivia," retorted Grandma Helen. "What in the world was I supposed to think?"

"Oh, I don't know, maybe that she had just returned home from visiting her daughter and Russian son-in-law in Toronto and was simply sharing all that she had learned about Russian cuisine?"

"Listen, this isn't about Mrs. Kramer or anyone else for that matter, this is about my daughter!" she snapped.

Mom immediately stopped what she was doing and looked questioningly over at Grandma Helen, "You really are worried about this, aren't you?"

Grandma Helen looked up at Mom with tears in her eyes, "You saw what he put her through, Olivia. He completely decimated her self-worth, made her feel like she was nothing, and acted like what he did wasn't a divorceable offense. He's been nothing but cavalier about the entire situation, and I for one, refuse to stand by and allow him to hurt her all over again; I simply won't do it."

"I had no idea you felt so strongly about all of this, Mom, I'm sorry if what I said hurt you," said Mom penitently.

"You and your sister mean more to me than anything else in this world, Olivia. There are no limitations to the things I will do to keep you protected and safe from harm, so if that means cutting that unbearable degenerate off at the pass, then I intend to do it." She walked over to the couch, kissed me on the forehead, and looked back over at Mom before heading toward the back door, "I'm 75 years old with ties to the mafia, my dear, that little pissant doesn't stand a snowball's chance in hell against me."

CHAPTER THREE

I must have fallen asleep right after Grandma Helen left because the next thing I knew, I was being stirred awake by the ear-splitting sound of Mom and Aunt Christine's hysterical laughter. The two of them always sounded like a pack of wild hyenas anytime they laughed together, so I knew there was no way I was getting back to sleep. I gingerly placed my hands on the sides of my protruding cheeks and immediately wished I hadn't. Although the pain was much more tolerable, the swelling was still significant, so in an effort to keep the pain under control, I immediately reached for three Tylenol and swallowed them down with a glass of water. I then nestled myself back under the blanket that Mom had placed over me and groggily listened as the two of them continued their cachinnations.

"It's a thousand stars from now on because they were so sweet and nice," I heard a voice slur incoherently. "I can give them my shoe for it, do you think they'd want my shoe?"

"No, honey, they don't want your shoe," answered a second voice.

"What do you mean they don't want my shoe?" the first voice wailed loudly. "Why don't they want my shoe, what's wrong with my shoe?"

"Nothing's wrong with your shoe, honey," the second voice stated calmly. "It's just that I think they'd rather you keep it, that's all."

"They're only twenty dollars on Amazon," the first voice garbled. "That's a great price for a knockoff, are you sure they don't want my shoe?"

As I sat quietly, listening to the two voices go back and forth discussing things that made absolutely no sense, I thought about the ice packs sitting in the freezer. I knew I needed to go and get them, but I was still half asleep with no desire to move, so instead, I continued to lay there with my eyes closed, letting the strange conversation envelop me.

"I know I shouldn't have said anything," the first voice continued. "They really are marvelous people, but they made me wait for so

15

long…and then the lady that was with me was really nice and made me feel so comfortable, I think I need to give her a hug."

"That's very sweet of you, honey, but I'm sure a simple 'thank you' will suffice," said the other voice.

"Do you think I've lost any weight from all this crying," asked the first voice.

"Honey, you don't have to lose weight," assured the second voice.

"But is it possible?"

"No."

"TikTok told me it was, though," said the first voice.

"Well, you can't believe everything you hear on TikTok, honey," said the second voice.

"But TikTok told me it was true!" wailed voice number one. "Wait, no, they said if you cry it makes your lashes longer, so maybe my lashes will be longer. Maybe they'll be…like…really, really long." There was a brief pause and then, "I bet I look just like a chimpanzee's ass right now, all red and swollen."

"I can assure you that you look nothing like a chimpanzee's ass," answered voice number two.

"You're lying!"

"I am not lying."

"And now there are four teeth missing from my mouth that I can never get back," the first voice wailed uncontrollably. "I'll never be able to get them back, Mom!"

"Oh, my God!" my eyes shot open.

I quickly jumped off the couch and ran into the kitchen, "Please tell me you did not post any of that on Facebook, Mother!" I tried unsuccessfully to grab the phone from her hands, but she was too quick, "Mom, please!"

"Would you calm down, Adelaide, I would never do something like that to you," scoffed Mom.

"Oh, really?" I crossed my arms and lifted my brow. "Because you had absolutely no problem posting that embarrassing doorbell footage of Ezra last week."

Last Tuesday, after a full day of studying for finals, Ezra had the misfortune of running into Mrs. Darby's psychopathic Doberman

Pincher, Mr. Peepers. He had apparently snuck out of her yard when she wasn't looking and had just finished wreaking havoc on our neighbor's azalea bushes when he caught sight of Ezra's car pulling into the driveway. Completely unaware that he was being stalked, Ezra casually retrieved his backpack from the backseat of the car and then immediately stopped short when he heard a low guttural growl emanating from behind him. Now, one thing to know about Mr. Peepers is that he does not like men and he especially does not like tall lanky shapes, so it's no surprise that at 6'8," Ezra made the perfect target.

Doing his best to not provoke the snarling and snapping dog more than he already had, Ezra slowly turned around to face his adversary. Realizing that he was in imminent danger, Ezra calmly backed away from the car and slowly made his way toward the front door, praying that he would make it before Mr. Peepers attacked. As he inched his way closer to the door, he thought back on something he had watched recently about scaring aggressive animals when passivity wasn't working, so in an effort to save himself, Ezra decided to give back just as good as he was getting and lunged toward the surly animal screaming and waving his arms around maniacally as he did. Mr. Peepers, who was completely caught off guard, tucked his tail between his legs and scurried away, crying and whimpering as if someone had just beaten him. Unfortunately, it was at this exact same moment that Mrs. Darby finally caught up with her wayward canine, and after witnessing the latter part of the encounter, immediately began scolding Ezra for scaring her poor baby into submission. Ezra then retaliated by calling Mr. Peepers a multitude of insults, one being that he was the canine equivalent of Hitler, before my father had to come outside and get involved. The entire exchange was not only caught and recorded on our Ring doorbell camera but was eventually made public via our mother's social media pages, so I'm sure you can imagine my concern.

"Hey, I got a lot of likes on that one!" she said defensively. "Besides, I owed him for stealing my Bluetooth speaker and dropping it in a bowl of queso."

"He dropped it in queso?" repeated Aunt Christine. "How in the world did he manage that?"

"I learned long ago not to ask questions you really don't want to know the answer to, so I honestly have no idea," answered Mom. She turned and retrieved two ice packs from the freezer and handed them over to me, "Anyway, I have no current plans to embarrass you on Facebook, or anywhere else for that matter, so please just go back to the couch and ice your face."

"You promise?" I asked apprehensively.

"I promise," she smiled.

I looked imploringly over at Aunt Christine, my face sandwiched between the two ice packs, "Please keep her away from Facebook."

"Don't worry, I've got this, honey," she winked. She watched as I slowly made my way back over to the couch and then turned back toward Mom, "Poor thing, I sure don't envy her right now." She plucked a Mandarin orange from the fruit bowl sitting on the counter and began to separate it from its peel, "Is she going to have enough time to heal before we leave for our trip?."

"The doctor seems to think she'll be back to normal in two or three days, so we should be all good." She leaned in close and lowered her voice, "You know, this trip to Italy couldn't have come at a better time, I'm really hoping it pulls her out of this slump she's in."

"She's in a mourning period, she'll eventually find her way out of it," said Aunt Christine.

This mourning period that Aunt Christine is referencing is really more of a dull ache now and is primarily due to a recent breakup I had with my boyfriend, Dusty. You see, a few weeks ago, my best friend, Skyler, reluctantly informed me that she had caught him cheating with a girl at their school named Shailyn Dupree. Shailyn, or rather Slutlyn, as Grandma Helen has so aptly rechristened her, apparently prides herself on her willingness and ableness to partake in a multitude of indiscretions, one being having sex with my boyfriend in the backseat of a car. Anyway, the minute I found out, I ended things, and despite his many attempts at trying to win me back, I refuse to give him the time of day. He even went so far as to approach me while I was out with Grandma Helen but realized rather quickly that she is even less forgiving than I am and has absolutely no problem making menacing threats in front of witnesses. Thankfully, he has since learned his lesson and has now opted to leave me alone.

"I'm actually really proud of how she handled herself," said Mom. "Heartbreak is never easy, but she wasn't about to let him weasel his way back into her life." She walked over to the refrigerator and opened the door, "Not to mention, I think Mom pretty much scared the crap out of him when she told him that she was willing to pay someone to castrate him in his sleep."

"She didn't," gasped Aunt Christine.

"Oh, she most certainly-" Mom stopped mid-sentence and pulled out an opened package of Polish Kielbasa, staring at it in complete disbelief, "You've got to be kidding me."

"What's wrong?" she asked.

Mom held up the package of Kielbasa and pointed to where a large chunk had recently been bitten out of it, "I bought this yesterday and I can assure you it did not look anything like this when I brought it home."

"Who would even do something like that?" asked Aunt Christine.

"It's either one of two people," she snarled. "And I'm fairly certain it's the one that's currently eating me out of house and home."

Mom was just about to pick up her phone when the culprit walked into the kitchen, "Hi Mom, hi Aunt Christine," smiled Ezra jovially.

"Please explain this to me," said Mom, pointing to the mangled piece of sausage resting in her hand. "I'd love to know why you felt it necessary to vandalize tonight's dinner."

"Oh yeah, I was wanting to see if Kielbasa tasted like Polish sausage since, you know, they look exactly alike," he shrugged.

"So you decided the best way to do that was to take a giant bite out of the unopened package sitting in the meat drawer?" she probed.

"It says it's precooked, so I figured it was safe to try," he answered.

"That doesn't mean you should eat it!" she shrieked. Mom took a deep calming breath and let it out slowly, "Ezra, did it ever occur to you that I purchased this for a reason; that maybe I was planning to use it for a meal?"

"Well, how was I supposed to know that?" he said defensively. "It was just sitting in the drawer."

"Oh gee, I don't know, maybe the fact that it was in an unopened package?" she snarked.

"Yeah, well, I open unopened packages of ham and turkey all the time and you never seem to freak out at me for doing that," he combated.

She looked at him as if he'd completely lost his mind, "We're not talking about lunch meat, son, we're talking about a 16-ounce bulk link of sausage."

"Oh, my God, I'm sorry, I'll go and get you some more," he said grabbing his keys.

"Yes, you will," she snapped back. "Oh and pick up another gallon of milk while you're at it."

"Yes ma'am," he sighed irritably.

"Ezra," she smiled feebly, "You know I love you, right?"

"Yes ma'am, I do," he grinned. "I love you too."

Mom set the half-eaten Kielbasa down on the counter and pulled out an onion along with two bell peppers from the refrigerator, "I tell you, raising kids is like being pecked to death by a chicken, excruciating and unrelenting."

"How did you even know it was him?" asked Aunt Christine.

Mom placed a cutting board on the counter and began chopping the peppers, "Ezra has always been curious when it comes to food. Whether it be winning combinations like an English muffin slathered in pepper and honey, Pringles and whipped cream, or sardines with mustard sauce, you had better believe that Ezra has either tried it or invented it."

"Ew, sardines in mustard sauce are absolutely disgusting," said Aunt Christine curling her lip.

"Yes, well, I blame his father for introducing him to that nastiness," said Mom. "Anyway, one day during Ezra's Sophomore year of high school, we had spent the morning discussing the differences between the Renaissance, Enlightenment, and Reformation periods of history. It was a very introspective discussion and I remember being in awe of all the connections he was making and the intelligent way in which he was speaking about the subject; I truly couldn't have been prouder." She sighed deeply before continuing, "That feeling, of course, quickly came to an end when I walked into the kitchen three hours later to find him tasting one of Churchill's dog treats to see if it actually tasted like bacon."

"You're kidding, right?" asked Aunt Christine.

"Unfortunately, no." She grabbed the onion sitting on the counter and sliced into it, "However, I did make him do a research paper on the way dog treats are made and that seemed to deter his curiosity in the matter." She finished slicing the onions and then rinsed her hands in the sink, "So, to answer your question, I would have to say that each of my children have their own calling card, and this one happens to be Ezra's."

CHAPTER FOUR

The next morning, I woke up feeling much more like myself and came downstairs to find mom and Beau sitting on the couch discussing *The Hiding Place*, a book by Corrie Ten Boom that chronicles her family's rescue of hundreds of Jews and Dutch resisters during the World War II Nazi invasion of Holland.

"So was the closet they were using to hide the Jews small?" asked Beau.

"It was very small and very compact," said mom. "In fact, it was probably similar in size to the closet you have in your room right now."

"You know, it's funny, but while I was reading that part, I couldn't stop imagining a big swirly slide that made its way from the upstairs closet down into a basement with a giant playground," said Beau. "Don't you think that would've been cool?"

"Well, I don't really think a playground in the basement would make much sense at a time when people were risking their lives to save persecuted Jews in occupied Holland, but it certainly makes for an interesting idea," said Mom. She took a deep breath and sighed mournfully, "You know, I can't even begin to fathom what those poor people went through. Imagine having to hide away for hours, and sometimes even days, stacked on top of each other like a can of sardines, never knowing whether or not you're going to make it out alive or even see your family again; It's truly a horrifying and debilitating thought."

"Hmm, I see your point," he nodded solemnly. "Maybe I was just using the whole swirly slide thing as some sort of coping mechanism, then."

"What do you mean by that?" asked Mom curiously.

"Oh, it's a strategy I tend to use anytime I need to maintain my mental and emotional well-being," he said. "Honestly, I use it a lot with Dad."

Why in the world would you need to use a coping mechanism with Dad" she asked confusedly.

"The man can literally take what should be a 10-minute punishment conversation and turn it into an hour-long disquisition simply because he refuses to stop repeating himself," he asserted. "All three of us have developed our own mechanisms. Ezra mentally alphabetizes his movie collection, Addie likes to sing songs in her head, and I like to think about swirly slides."

"Huh, I had no idea that you did that, but I suppose I can see your point," said Mom. She closed the book and reached for her coffee, "Listen, we'll pick this back up tomorrow since that's going to be our last day of school before we leave, and it'll also enable you to get your math test done before lunch."

"Ugh, math," he grumbled. "And what happens if I don't do well on this test?"

"You'll do just fine; your math has improved a lot," she said encouragingly.

"Yeah, but what if I don't do well?" he asked.

"Then you'll retake the test," she answered.

"And what happens if I don't do well on that one?" he pressed.

"Just put a repetend over my last statement and you'll know exactly what happens," said Mom as she made her way into the kitchen.

"I'm sorry, but I don't understand math speak," he combated.

"Well, then maybe we need to add a math vocabulary to your daily lessons," she shot back. "I'm sure that'll help you get up to speed in no time."

"Geez, there's no need to get persnickety, Mom, I'll just go and take the test, okay?" He picked up his backpack and headed upstairs, "I was finally able to use that word in a sentence, I am seriously awesome!"

"And the reason I drink," she mumbled quietly to herself. She walked over to the where I was sitting and wrapped her arms around me, "Hey baby, how are you feeling?"

"I'm actually feeling a lot better," I said. "The swelling is almost completely gone and the pain isn't anywhere near as bad as it was yesterday."

"Well, let's not take any chances, shall we?" She kissed the back of my head and then handed me three Tylenol along with a glass of water, "You're probably going to need to keep up with this for another day, at least."

"Yes, ma'am," I said.

Mom walked into the pantry and pulled out a bag of fresh bagels, "How about I make you bagel with cream cheese and strawberry jam, I know how much you love those."

"That'd be great, Mom, thanks," I smiled.

"So, what are your plans for the day?" she asked.

"I think Skylar is going to come over later and help me figure out some outfits for Italy, but other than that, I'm fairly free," I said.

"Aren't you glad you took my advice and finished your finals early?" asked Mom, slicing the bagel and placing it in the toaster, "I only wish your brother had heeded that same advice, then I could be done with everything too."

"Does he even have that much left?" I asked.

"Honestly, no, he doesn't, but he certainly isn't aware of that," she said. "I swear, that child doesn't know if he's coming or going anytime it comes to school; hell, half the time he doesn't even know what month it is. Quite frankly, I think the only month he even pays attention to is October because of his birthday, otherwise, he lives in a vacuum whereby June could be January as far as he's concerned."

"Good morning, my darlings!" trilled Grandma Helen, waltzing in through the back door. "Let's go have a day of shopping, shall we?"

"Again?" asked Mom incredulously. "We just went shopping this past Sunday."

"And your point would be?" she queried.

"My point is that we have a very expensive trip to Italy coming up in four days and probably don't need to be spending any extra money," answered Mom.

"Yes, dear, I know," said Grandma Helen. "I was the one who bought the tickets and paid for the hotels, remember?" She reached behind Mom to grab a coffee mug, "Anyway, I've decided that I need to find a nice wool wrap to keep me warm at night, preferably in emerald, green, since I look so fabulous in that color." She picked up the coffee pot and poured a generous amount into her mug, "And then I thought we'd go and visit Justin at the bistro for lunch since I told him I would make it a point to come by and see him before we left for our trip." She poured some cream into her coffee, "And I'd just hate to disappoint him, you know how much he looks forward to seeing me."

"You sure about that?" asked Mom dubiously.

"Of course I'm sure, he's said so, himself," she said irritably. "Not to mention the fact that he's always asking me questions like when he can expect to see me again, how long I'm planning to stay for lunch, whether or not I'm planning on entertaining the idea of an after-dinner cordial or dessert." She slowly sipped her coffee, "Honestly, if I didn't know any better I'd think he had a little crush on me."

"The man has literally developed a nervous tick ever since you started requesting his table, Mother, so I'm pretty sure those little queries are more about mental preparation than anything else." She took a plate out of the cabinet and set it on the counter, "And let's not forget how flamboyantly gay he is."

"Oh, don't be ridiculous, Olivia, the man adores me," she scoffed. "And I'm well aware of the fact that he's gay, I was just making a point."

"Okay, if you say so," she shrugged.

Mom retrieved the warm bagel from the toaster, slathered it in cream cheese and strawberry jam, and then handed it over to me, "Oh, by the way, Ezra took my car to get serviced today, so I'm not going be able to drive."

"That's alright, dear, I'll drive," said Grandma Helen. She sipped her coffee and pointedly fixed her gaze on me, "Oh, darling, I do hope you're planning on brushing your hair at some point today and maybe putting on a little blush, you look peaked."

"I just woke up, Grandma," I said defensively.

"A lady should always look her best no matter what time of day," she asserted. "But at least you no longer look like death warmed over, so I suppose that's progress."

"Gee, you're too kind," I grumbled, biting into my bagel.

Just then Dad marched into the kitchen with a scowl on his face as he handed an Xbox controller over to Mom, "This is ours until Monday."

"Uh oh, what did he do now?" she asked.

"I just went in to check in on him, and rather than doing his schoolwork like he is supposed to be doing, he was playing that stupid *Snow Runner* game.

"Oh no, that's not good," she winced. "Did he have anything to say for himself?"

"Uh, oops," he imitated irritably.

Dad poured himself a cup of coffee and stared over at Mom, "I'm serious, Olivia, good behavior isn't going to win it back this time. I'm sick of this happening, so unless he saves a baby or something, it's gone." He grabbed a banana and granola bar before heading back to his office, "And he doesn't need to be playing hours of video games every week either. He can go play basketball with Tyler, work on a model plane, knit grass blades into a hat, I don't care, but he doesn't need to be playing those games as often as he does."

"I agree," nodded Mom. "Let me just finish figuring out the plan for today and I'll go and have a talk with him."

"Thank you," he said kissing her cheek. "Listen, I have to go and get on a work call, but we'll discuss this more later, okay?"

"Yes, of course." She placed the lids back on the cream cheese and jam and sighed, "I swear that child is going to be the death of me."

"Oh, come now, you said the same thing about Ezra, darling, and yet here you are, living the dream with a fully stocked wine bar," said Grandma Helen cheerfully.

"Yes, well, the wine certainly does seem to help," she admitted.

Mom began putting a few of the breakfast items away and immediately stopped short when she noticed Churchill, our entitled and very pretentious English Bulldog staring expectantly up at her.

"Oh no, Mommy forgot to feed you, didn't she?" She quickly ran into the laundry room, grabbed his dog bowl, and filled it with food, "I can't believe I forgot to feed my sweet baby boy."

I looked up at the clock, "You're only thirty minutes late, Mom, I think he'll live."

"Oh, you poor baby, you must be starving." She hastily mixed the vitamin supplements, Alaskan salmon oil, and pumpkin puree into his food and lovingly placed it down in front of him, "Here you go, precious, I'm so sorry to have made you wait."

"Tell me, dear, why exactly is his dog bowl shaped like a little circular rodent maze?" asked Grandma Helen curiously.

"Oh, that's to keep him from eating too fast," said Mom. She filled Churchill's water bowl with fresh water and set it down next to him, "In fact, it not only slows down his eating, but also acts as a fun little puzzle to keep his brain engaged, so in addition to aiding with his digestion, it also helps with his brain function."

Churchill gave Mom an irritated side eye, coughed up some regurgitated food, and then immediately reclaimed it.

"Yes, well, you may want to think about getting your money back for that one," said Grandma Helen curling her lip.

"He has acid reflux and a delicate stomach, so sometimes that happens," said Mom defensively. "And I'm sure he doesn't enjoy doing that any more than you enjoy seeing it, so how about we give him a little bit of grace, okay?"

"He's a dog, darling, not royalty," snickered Grandma Helen.

"Come on Churchy, let's go potty," said Mom, ignoring the slight.

"I seriously cannot believe you let that animal defecate all over the back lawn," snarled Grandma Helen. "It's like traversing the streets of San Francisco every time I walk to and from my house."

"Okay, first of all, that's gross," said Mom, gently plucking a wet wipe from a plastic container on the counter, "Secondly, it's cleaned up daily, and thirdly, how would you even know, you've never even stepped foot in San Francisco."

"I don't need to, dear, I watch the news," she sniffed haughtily. "Besides, I don't think I'd fare too well in a vagrant laden society that unabashedly uses its public streets as a toilet; I do have standards, you know."

"Wait a minute, is that a wipe warmer?" I asked in disbelief. "Did you seriously buy that dog a wipe warmer?"

"I did, yes," smiled Mom. "The wipes were cold, damp, and uncomfortable, so I figured he'd like to have one."

"He's a dog, Mom, he doesn't care," I said.

"He does too care," she said indignantly. "In fact, he's much more amenable to going outside now, and I attribute that to having a nice warm wipe waiting for him when he's finished."

"Wait a minute, you mean to tell me that you actually wipe that animals—" Grandma Helen's next words were immediately cut off by her phone dinging, alerting her to an incoming text. She quickly read over it and then immediately walked over to the sink, "You're father needs me come home and help him with something," she said rinsing out her cup. "Can the two of you be ready in about an hour?"

"I don't think that should be a problem," said Mom opening the back door. "I just need to make sure I have a little chat with Beau before we leave." She bent down and gently wiped Churchill's backside, "How about I give you a call when we're ready?"

"Ugh, I can't believe you're actually doing that, Olivia," snarled Grandma Helen, repulsively sidestepping around them. "Surely there must be some sort of alternative; a bidet, perhaps?"

"He can't help it, Mom," she said, folding the wipe and dropping it in the outside trash can, "And, seeing as he has absolutely no idea how to operate a toilet, I can't imagine he'll have much more luck with a bidet, but by all means, keep the suggestions coming."

"Well maybe you should look into hiring that little dog whisperer TV man and he can train him to use one," said Grandma Helen.

"Cesar Milan is an incredibly busy man, Mother, but I'll be sure to call him first thing tomorrow morning and see if I can't set something up," snarked Mom. She closed the door, walked straight into the kitchen, and washed her hands, "Only your grandmother would recommend hiring Cesar Milan to train a dog to use an outdoor bidet." She grabbed a towel and began drying her hands, "I tell you, that woman has serious issues, Addie."

"Says the woman that just bought her dog a wipe warmer," I muttered quietly.

"Would you stop?" said Mom. "Churchill deserves a little pampering too, especially with us leaving him behind for a full two weeks."

"You literally spend ten minutes warming up the car before taking him to his vet appointments, splurge on special food and treats, pay an obscene amount of money for allergy shots, and regularly buy him toys he continues to ignore." I put my plate in the dishwasher and rinsed out my coffee cup, "That dog's life is the epitome of champagne wishes and caviar dreams, and now you're telling me he has a wipe warmer for his butt too?"

Mom reached for another warm wipe and began cleaning the folds on Churchill's face, "They're actually multi-functional, honey, but yes, it would seem that he does," she smirked.

CHAPTER FIVE

An hour later I found myself in the backseat of Grandma Helen's Mercedes, holding on for dear life as she carelessly weaved her way in and out of downtown traffic. The incessant honking and vulgar finger gestures hurled her way did absolutely nothing to deter her, and rather than heed my warnings to either slow down or maybe stay in one lane, she simply sped along as if she hadn't a care in the world. My mother, who would normally be having an absolute conniption right about now, saw none of this as she was currently having to deal with yet another unwanted phone call from her eldest offspring.

"What now, Ezra?" shouted Mom into the phone.

"Geez, Mom, you don't have to be so rude," he said defensively.

"Ezra, this is the fifth time you've called me in less than ten minutes. I know you're bored; I know you're frustrated with the little girl who won't stop singing, I know you don't care for their meager offering of snack foods, and I'm well aware of the fact that you hate having to forcibly watch the Food Network while sitting in the waiting room, but you cannot keep calling me every time the tiniest little thing begins to irk you."

One thing to know and understand about Ezra is that Mom is pretty much his best friend. He calls her about everything under the sun, and although he would never openly admit to such a thing, his actions and daily call logs tend to tell another story. So, where you and I might choose to bend the ear of a best friend or a significant other, Ezra likes to moan, whine, and lodge every single complaint, thought, or opinion he has to our mother. She has quite literally become his therapist, advisor, and sounding board all wrapped up into one, and if I'm being completely honest, I think she's ready for someone else to take over the reins, namely

Sabrina, his girlfriend of over a year. And even though she may daydream about the one day she'll finally be able to hand over that torch, she knows, just like the rest of us, that this is her cross to bear, and probably will be until her dying day.

"Okay, I understand," he said penitently. "But Mom, you would not believe the utter contempt that some of these judges have toward the contestants on this show. For example, this woman, Marina, literally just made a six-foot multi-story house completely out of chocolate with a ganache-covered roof, and one of the judges had the audacity to tell her it was unsightly and grotesque. I mean, show a little respect for God's sake."

"Ezra," said Mom calmly. 'Please don't call me again unless it has something to do with my car."

"Oh, your car's fine," he said. "The oil's been changed and they said everything looks good."

"Wait, so you're telling me that they've already finished with my car?" she clarified.

"Yeah, about five minutes ago," he answered.

"Then what are you even still doing there?" she asked.

"Mom, I really don't think you're understanding the magnitude of Marina's talent," he combatted. "The woman literally just designed and manufactured a man-sized house made entirely out of chocolate, and I don't care what any of those judges say, that takes skill and should be acknowledged as such."

"Goodbye, Ezra," said Mom.

"Wait, no 'I love you'?" he asked incredulously.

"I love you," she said.

"I love you too," he said.

Mom hung up the phone and placed it in her purse just as Grandma Helen abruptly swung into a parking place. "Time to go shopping!" she announced flamboyantly.

"Thank God," I muttered, trying to regain the feeling in my fingers, "I don't think I could have handled much more of that."

We exited the car and began making our way to the front entrance of Macy's when Mom immediately stopped short and said, "You can't possibly be serious with this."

"Serious with what, dear?" asked Grandma Helen.

Mom pointed to the single white line that Grandma Helen's Mercedes was currently straddling, "You aren't even remotely inside the lines, Mother, you can't leave it like this."

"I park like this all the time, darling," dismissed Grandma Helen. "It's honestly fine."

"Have you completely lost your mind?" asked Mom. "What about all the other people that want to park here? They're not going to be able to because you're taking up two spots."

Grandma Helen slowly looked around the empty parking lot while making it a point to press the lock button on her key fob, "I really don't see that being an issue, dear." She then turned and began walking toward the entrance of the store, "Besides, the parking here would be so much easier if each spot were at a slant, I do much better with those. Having to maneuver my way in and out of these rigid sideways parking spaces is an incredibly daunting task, and if I'm being completely honest, I'd rather not have to worry about it."

"Rigid sideways parking spaces?" repeated Mom. "Okay, that's it, I'm telling Dad you don't need to be driving anymore."

"You will do no such thing!" she spat.

"Mom, you can't even park your car between the lines of a parking space when no other cars are present, that really doesn't elicit much confidence in your ability as a driver," said Mom.

"I am perfectly capable of parking my car in these spaces, Olivia," said Grandma Helen. "I just choose not to spend precious time doing it."

"Well, I still think Dad should know this information," said Mom. "Especially after that whole parking ticket controversy from last year."

"And I think Greg should know that you're the one that drank the last of his Caymus Reserve Cabernet while binge-watching *Bridgerton* the last time he was out of town," she retaliated."

"You wouldn't dare!" gasped Mom.

"You tell your father about any of this and yes, I most certainly would dare," she challenged.

"Wait, you watch *Bridgerton*?" I asked confusedly. "You and Dad told me it was complete trash and that I should stay away from it."

"No, your father said it was complete trash," she clarified. "I said that it was an absurdly inaccurate take on the Regency era of London and that it incorrectly presented the societal realities found within the differing classes and races prominent during that particular time in history, and yes, I agree, you should definitely stay away from it."

"And don't forget about the porn, dear," added Grandma Helen.

"It's not porn, Mother," said Mom.

"I've watched the show, darling, and it most is certainly porn." She mindlessly twirled the keyring in her hand, "At least part of the time."

"Ew," I curled my lip.

"You know what, fine, just give me the damn keys and I'll move it," snapped Mom.

"I don't know why you're acting so upset, dear, you're the one that chose to watch scandalous television and secretly knock back an extremely expensive bottle of wine while your husband was away," shrugged Grandma Helen.

"I'm upset because we wouldn't even be having this conversation if you would just stop being lazy and learn to park like a normal person," answered Mom. "You have absolutely no respect for other people and are incredibly short-sighted whenever it comes to simple common courtesy.

"There's no need to sling insults, Olivia," she bristled. "I just didn't think it was that big of a deal since no one else is really here."

Mom made a show of extending her hand, "The keys please, Mother."

Grandma Helen finally acquiesced and watched as Mom stomped irritably back over to the car.

"Please be careful with Cecilia, darling, she's very precious to me," she called out.

"You named your car Cecilia?" I asked.

"Yes," she said. "I named her after one of Simon and Garfunkel's greatest hits. It always seemed like such a happy peppy song, and since Cecilia is my peppy little sidekick, it seemed fitting."

"I'm not familiar with the song," I said.

"Well, we shall remedy that soon enough on the way home, my darling," she lovingly patted my cheek.

Once Mom had finished moving the car and we were finally nearing the entrance to Macy's, Grandma Helen stopped short, "Did you remember to move Cecilia's seat back into the correct position?"

"No, I didn't, I'm sorry," said Mom.

"But she doesn't like that; she's very particular, you know," she combated.

"I think she'll live, Mother," said Mom, rolling her eyes. She then opened the front door and added, "You know, I honestly don't know how someone hasn't keyed your car already, it would be well deserved."

"Well, it's certainly fine if they do, darling," she smiled flippantly. "I'll just simply look into having it repainted, I'm thinking I may be ready for a color change anyway."

***

The next four days went by rather quickly, and before we knew it, the day of our departure was finally upon us. Believe it or not, the six of us, including Mom and Aunt Christine, were able to pack everything we needed into two carry-ons each, a feat I wasn't even quite sure would be possible, let alone feasible. However, thanks to my mother's incessant weekly packing drills over the last month, we were able to do just that. Knowing full well that my grandmother is not only incapable, but unwilling, to travel without at least half her wardrobe, and also knowing that in her world, the notion of repeating an outfit is not only ludicrous, but offensive, my mother thought it prudent for the rest of us to pack as lightly as possible. You see, Grandma Helen's propensity to overpack will inevitably render itself to at least one or more of us having to lug her bags up and down the multitude of steps and cobblestone pathways that make up Italy, and rather than struggle over a difficult terrain that doesn't lend itself to an overabundance of luggage, Mom thought it best to just keep it simple.

"Does anyone have any idea how many bags your grandmother is bringing?" asked Dad, loading the car. "I figure that woman's luggage is going to make my life a living hell over the next few weeks, so I may as well brace myself now."

"Yeah, well, you're not the only one," said Beau. "Grandpa Anthony's already pulled me and Ezra aside and told us that we would basically be the human equivalent of a pack mule going forward, so you're not going to get any sympathy from me."

"He did not call you a pack mule, Beau," I scoffed. "He just said that the two of you need to be ready to help everyone with their luggage, that's all."

Beau held up both hands as if to mimic a balance scale, "Help with luggage, pack mule, they're pretty much one and the same, if you ask me."

"And you're an idiot, if you ask me," I retorted.

"Seriously, do either one of you know how many bags your grandmother is bringing?" asked Dad irritably. "I need to know If I can make all of this fit."

"I think Mom said she was finally able to limit it down to two, but I wouldn't hold my breath on that one," I said.

Dad continued shifting things around, literally playing *Tetris* with the luggage, "Alright, well, I think I should be able to get two more bags in here." He then wiped the sweat from his brow and asked, "Where is your mother, anyway?"

"She's currently laying on the floor trying to console Churchill," I answered. "She's apparently deluded herself into thinking he's going to miss her."

"Oh, dear God, you can't be serious," he rolled his eyes. "As long as that dog is being fed, he could care less who's there to do it." He looked down and checked the time on his watch, "Listen, we really need to get a move on, can one of you please go and see what's keeping your grandparents?"

"Here I am, darling!" trilled Grandma Helen merrily. "Anthony's right behind me, but I think he might need a little help with our things."

"Beau, can you please go and see about helping your grandfather?" asked Dad.

"Oh, great, it's already starting," muttered Beau. "Maybe I should just grab a pannier bag and a few sling ropes while I'm at it."

"Whatever you need, darling, just be sure that none of it touches my Louis Vuitton luggage," called out Grandma Helen. She then amiably turned her attention over to Dad, "I'll have you to know that I was quite diligent in my packing methods for this trip, Gregory, and even cast aside four crucial outfits in order to make it all work."

"You're a true humanitarian, Helen," mumbled Dad.

Before she had a chance to respond, Mom and Aunt Christine slowly approached the car. "Don't worry, Bryan is going to take excellent care of Churchill," soothed Aunt Christine. "He's rearranged his entire schedule in order to spend as much quality time as possible with him."

"It does really help to know that he'll be staying here and keeping him company while we're away," sniffed Mom. "I just don't want Churchy to feel like we've abandoned him."

"The dog literally just walked away from you for a Snausage, Mom," said Ezra following closely behind. "You need to open your eyes and see him for what he truly is, a canine glutton."

As we all began to pile into the car, Beau sidled up to Dad, tapped him on the shoulder, and silently presented the last of the luggage.

"Three suitcases?" he hissed. "Are you kidding me?"

"You can't possibly be telling me you're surprised by any of this," said Beau drolly. "I really thought you were smarter than that."

"She literally just stood there and told me that she was diligent in her packing and even omitted outfits to make it work," said Dad. "I have absolutely no idea how I'm supposed to make all of this fit."

"Mistake number one was taking Grandma at her word," said Beau. "The rest of us know not to do that."

"Well, you could have at least warned me," said Dad.

"I was hoping she'd turn over a new leaf, but apparently I was mistaken," quipped Beau.

Dad walked over to the side of the van where Grandma Helen and Grandpa Anthony were standing, "Anthony, I have absolutely no idea how I'm going to make those three suitcases fit."

"Maybe you could strap one of them to the roof," offered Beau congenially.

"No, absolutely not," asserted Grandma Helen. "It's Louis Vuitton! You do not defile and desecrate Louis Vuitton luggage by tying it to a luggage rack, what is wrong with you?"

"Actually, that may not be a bad idea, Beau," said Dad.

"Over my dead body!" exclaimed Grandma Helen.

"Yeah, well, I'm pretty sure that can be arranged, Helen," muttered Dad as he turned to go and grab some rope from the garage.

CHAPTER SIX

Needless to say, Grandma Helen was alive and well when we finally arrived at the airport, and although I'm not entirely sure if it was due to Dad's hesitancy to spend the rest of his life in prison or simply because she was the one holding everyone's airline tickets hostage, he decided to choose the path of least resistance and give her a stay of execution. More importantly, he was able to salvage her precious luggage from being "defiled and desecrated" by the roof of our pristine two-month-old Cadillac Escalade.

The drive down to the airport was a relatively uneventful one, and after a short shuttle ride from the parking area over to the main terminal, we eventually found ourselves through security and on our way over to the international concourse.

"Ugh, why did we have to get here so early?" grumbled Beau. "Our plane doesn't even leave for three hours; this is going to be so boring."

Yes, well, ensuring that the eight of us can actually make it to the same place at the same time takes sacrifice, Beau" said Mom. "But not to worry, I'm sure you'll have the emotional strength to survive the ordeal, you're only 13 after all."

"Your mother's right, dear," chirped Grandma Helen happily as she rolled her carry-on next to him. "I have absolutely no doubt that you'll live to tell the tale of your excruciating three-hour wait to board a plane for an all-expenses-paid two-week vacation to Italy." She then moved past him and added, "Think of it as a harrowing survival story you'll be able to pass down to your children and grandchildren like those of a decorated war veteran."

"Oh snap, Grandma," laughed Ezra. "That was savage!"

"Shut up, Ezra," spat Beau.

"I'm not quite sure what any of that means, darling, but I'll take it as a compliment." She then sped up and made her way over to Mom and Aunt Christine, "I don't know about the two of you, but I think we should all head over to the airport lounge and relax with a few preflight drinks."

"You're certainly not going to get any argument out of me," said Mom. "I'm all about a preflight cocktail."

"Nor me," answered Aunt Christine.

"Wonderful!" exclaimed Grandma Helen. She then hurried over to where Dad and Grandpa Anthony were walking, "Boys, I think we've decided that we'd all like to go and have a few cocktails while we wait for the plane to arrive."

"Already planning on slamming a few back, are we, dear?" snarked Grandpa Anthony.

"Vacation starts the minute I get through security, Anthony, you know this about me," she pronounced proudly.

"That I do, my love," he laughed.

"You know, I think I read somewhere that there's one of those Chase priority lounges here in the international terminal," said Mom. "Maybe we can go there."

"It's actually just up the way," answered Dad, slowly coming to a stop. "In fact, why don't all of you stay here with the luggage while Anthony and I go and check it out."

"That would be divine, dear, thank you," smiled Grandma Helen. She then turned her attention over to Mom and Aunt Christine beaming with excitement, "This way the three of us can get Italy-ready together!"

Mom cocked her head in confusion, "I'm not sure I'm following."

"Well, you and Christine have been saying for weeks now that the two of you were getting 'Italy-ready,' so I just figured we'd continue with the festivities while waiting here at the airport," she shrugged.

"Mom, you do know that we were talking about exercise right?" said Aunt Christine.

"Exercise?" she gasped. "Why on earth would you ever want to do that?"

"Oh, I don't know, maybe to improve our health, longevity, and quality of life," mused Mom.

"Or maybe to physically prepare themselves to drag all of your luggage up and down the cobbled streets of every city we visit?" muttered Beau inaudibly.

"Well, that's not any fun," pouted Grandma Helen. "I had rather hoped that the two of you were working on your tolerance levels for all the wine we'll be drinking."

Ezra leaned in conspiratorially, "After decades of tireless practice, I'd say they both pretty much have a corner on that market, Grandma."

"Don't you have some other place to hover, Ezra?" asked Mom irritably.

"Nah, I'm all good," he smirked. "But please let me know if I can be of any further assistance."

"You know, exercise has never really appealed to me," sniffed Grandma Helen. "And even if it did, I certainly wouldn't let it trump the proper way to get 'Italy-ready,'" She leaned over to see what was keeping Dad and Grandpa Anthony, "Not to mention it's incredibly difficult to find the time with my busy schedule; I do have priorities, you know."

"And what, pray tell, has you so occupied that you can't even carve out an hour to take a nice walk?" asked Mom.

"Okay, first of all, I don't walk, Olivia, I shop," she clarified. "Secondly, I have plenty of things to occupy my time. She began ticking off her fingers, "There's my nights at the theater, directorial and production meetings, lunch at the bistro, my charitable outlets…"

"What charitable outlets?" interrupted Mom. "You hate charity."

"Yeah, Mom, the only time you've ever done anything for charity was last Christmas when you begrudgingly helped Joan coordinate the Angel Tree," said Aunt Christine. "And even that was only because you thought you were going to be featured on WXBTV news."

"You know what, never mind," she snapped. "Let's just drop the unpleasantness of the subject and chalk it up to the fact that I haven't the time, the will, nor the desire, to get hot, sweaty, and nasty, alright?"

"Well, I really think you may want to start making the time, Mom," said Aunt Christine. "You may find that it actually does you some good, especially now that you're getting older."

"I'm sorry, darling, but have you seen my figure?" snickered Grandma Helen. "I look better now than I did 30 years ago, and my doctor has not only given me a perfect bill of health but he's also said I'm likely to live at least another 20 years."

"Oh, great," muttered Beau, "Another 20 years of unadulterated bliss."

"That's enough," mouthed Mom angrily.

"Okay everyone, we have tables!" interjected Dad cheerfully. "And there's more than enough room for us to store all of the luggage too, so follow me."

The airport lounge was a welcome reprieve from the busyness of the outside terminal. It was a relaxing space with plenty of tables and very few people, so it was no surprise to find a tranquil-looking Grandpa Anthony happily sipping bourbon as we stepped through the front door. He was nestled inside the confines of an overly large brown leather chair when Grandma Helen, who by this time was in dire need of a spirited refreshment, plopped down unceremoniously next to him and said, "I need a drink."

"Not to worry, my darling, your Prosecco's on the way," he said, gently patting her hand.

"Ugh, a bar," sighed Beau. "Why am I not surprised?" He walked over to a nearby table and took a seat, "I tell you; these people take merriment to a whole new level."

I sat down next to him and pointed to the long rectangular table lined with multiple chafing dishes, "All is not lost, dear brother, I think I see chicken wings over there."

"Oh, sweet, a buffet!" he exclaimed excitedly. He then jumped up and immediately headed over to where the food was, "You know, this may not be such a waste of time after all."

One thing to know about Beau is that his greatest happiness in life can be found at an all-you-can-eat buffet. So much so, that he emphatically promotes the Golden Corral as his all-time favorite restaurant, not because the food is good, because let's be honest, it's not, but rather because he likes the idea of scarfing down as much food as possible for the very low price of $12.99. In fact, he has even issued himself a personal challenge any time we dine there (once annually for his birthday) to overindulge so much that the manager has no choice but to ask him to stop eating and vacate the premises, an idea that came to him shortly after watching a man get kicked out of an all-you-can-eat Chinese buffet on TikTok.

"Oh, dear God," said Mom, watching Beau set down two large plates of food. "Please tell me you've left a little something for everyone else."

"Well, you know the carrots and celery are never going to find their way to my plate, so those are obviously still there, but as for everything else…well, you snooze, you lose," he shrugged.

"Son, you need to learn that there's a certain code of conduct when it comes to buffets," said Dad pointedly. "And piling five pounds of chicken wings onto a plate is not one of them."

"Actually, I have two plates," he grinned innocently.

"You know exactly what you're father means, Beau, so don't get smart," said Mom.

"Okay, fine, I understand," he answered penitently. "But in my defense, I would like to point out that I was left unsupervised, and as we all know, that tends to come with consequences."

"Yes, you do seem to be the gift that keeps on giving, dear," snarked Grandma Helen.

Before Beau had the chance to respond in kind, I decided to step in and change the subject, "So, Dad, is this a lounge you come to very often?"

"No, I don't, actually," he shook his head. "I primarily fly domestic, so I'm usually over in that terminal."

"Aren't you also a Delta Gold member since you fly so much?" asked Ezra.

"I have Gold Medallion status, yes," he said.

"What makes gold status so great?" asked Beau, his hands dripping with wing sauce.

"Beau where's your napkin?" asked Mom.

"I'm wearing it," he said sarcastically, licking his fingers. "Napkin shirts seem to be all the rage right now, so I figured I'd give one a try."

Dad reached over, placed a black cloth napkin in front of him, and cleared his throat, "Having gold status comes with a lot of different perks that make flying more enjoyable for those of us who do it a lot."

"What kind of perks?" he asked.

"Well, in this case, it'll help me board the plane before all of you and may even result in an upgrade to first class," he said.

"You wouldn't dare!" exclaimed Grandma Helen.

"I don't know, Helen, if I get upgraded to Delta One, I may just have to leave the rest of you in the dust," he grinned.

"Darling, if you get upgraded to Delta One, that seat will be going directly to me," she combated.

"You know, it's funny," mused Aunt Christine. "It doesn't matter how many times I fly; I still get nervous about missing my flight." She grabbed a few pretzels off Beau's plate, "I mean, I'm literally sitting here with a perfect view of our gate, and I'm still worried we're going to miss it."

"I can assure you that we won't miss it, honey," said Grandpa Anthony. "We have plenty of time, and like you said, we are literally sitting across from the gate."

"I know," she sighed. "The rational side of me knows this, but it still causes me great anxiety nonetheless."

"That's what causes you great anxiety?" asked Mom. "I would have thought it would be running out of wine."

"No, that's your issue," she laughed.

"Well, for me, it's going through airport security," said Beau. He took a bite out of his last chicken wing, "Every single time I have to walk through that metal detector, I can't help but think to myself, 'What happens if I accidentally have a gun?'"

"You're an idiot," said Ezra.

"Hey, it's been known to happen," he said.

"Yeah, like when?" I asked.

"Like when my friend, Kyle, said that his Uncle Danny accidentally forgot to take off his carry weapon when he and his wife were going to Hawaii for their second honeymoon. He was immediately detained, questioned for hours, and missed his flight." Beau wiped his mouth with his napkin, "And I have absolutely no intention of repeating his error."

"Yeah, well, last time I checked, they don't give guns to morons, so I'm pretty sure you don't have anything to worry about," said Ezra.

While Beau and Ezra bantered back and forth about gun issuance and the people least likely to receive one, I immediately turned my attention over to Grandma Helen, who had quietly been sipping her Prosecco and scrutinizing Mom's carry-on luggage.

"You know, dear, you may want to think about replacing your un-matched Target luggage with something a little bit nicer," she said, raising a brow.

"It's functional, Mother, and works just fine," said Mom. "And for the record, it's not from Target."

"Okay, well your Walmart luggage, then," she sniffed haughtily.

"It's not from Walmart, either," said Mom.

"Goodwill?" she pressed.

"Stop being obnoxious, Mother," said Mom. "You know perfectly well that it came from the Samsonite store, you were there when I bought it."

"And when exactly was that, dear, 1989?" asked Grandma Helen.

Ignoring the slight, Mom immediately leaned over to Aunt Christine and said, "I'll seriously pay you $500 to switch seats with me."

"No way," she shook her head.

"I would do it for you!" hissed Mom.

"No, you wouldn't," laughed Aunt Christine.

"Okay, how about $1000?" asked Mom.

"Sorry, I can't be bought," she answered. "Besides, there isn't enough money in the world to ever get me to willingly sit in that seat."

"Ugh, I can't say I blame you," muttered Mom, sipping her drink, "Well, can you at least tell me how long we need to be in the air before the flight attendant brings the beverage cart?"

"Probably thirty or forty minutes, give or take," said Aunt Christine.

"Well, let's just pray it's more take than give because I don't think I can handle sitting next to that woman sober," sighed Mom.

CHAPTER SEVEN

"I still don't understand why Ezra gets to sit all the way up there with Dad and Grandpa while I have to sit all the way back here," pouted Beau. He crossed his arms petulantly. "This is so unfair."

"It's not like you've been seated in the depths of hell, Beau, they're only two rows ahead of us," said Mom, rolling her eyes. "And besides, it wasn't anything personal, it was simply strategic."

We hadn't been on the plane fifteen minutes before Beau launched into his tirade about the unfairness of his seat relegation. Trying to find eight seats together was practically impossible, so we had to make do with what we were given. Ezra, Dad, and Grandpa Anthony were a few rows up to the left, while Aunt Christine sat by herself a few rows back on the right. Grandma Helen, Mom, Beau, and I were all seated together directly in the middle, and Beau was completely indignant about it.

"Yeah, but why does Ezra get to be up there?" he said. "It's not like he's the fun one."

"Because he's 6'8" and needs the legroom," answered Mom. She casually turned the page of her magazine, "And I'm not entirely sure many in the family would agree with that last statement."

"I certainly wouldn't," muttered Grandma Helen under her breath.

"Can I at least sit there on the flight back?" he persisted.

"No," she answered plainly.

"Why not?" he moaned.

"Because you and I both know that you have no business taking on the responsibilities that come with sitting in an exit row," she replied.

"Hey, you don't know that," he said.

"Yes, I do," she said matter-of-factly.

"Well, it can't be that hard if Ezra's sitting there," he snarked. "What exactly would I have to do, anyway?"

Mom put down her magazine and peered over at him, "Well, first of all, you'll need to pay rapt attention to the flight attendant during the pre-flight announcement. Then you'll need to agree to…"

"Okay, let me just stop you there," he said, raising his hands in surrender. "I do enough listening in school, I don't need to listen to someone in uniform drone on and on about inflight safety during my vacation." He reached down into his backpack and took out a bag of gummy bears, "Besides, the likelihood of us crashing into the ocean is slim to none, and since I'm literally sitting on a floatation device, I think I'm pretty much covered." He opened up the bag and then looked over at me, "Do you think there's any chance Aunt Christine would be willing to trade seats with me?"

"I don't think so," I said, shaking my head. "She was pretty quick to shoot Mom down even after she offered to pay a hefty sum for it." I reached into his bag of gummy bears, "And considering the fact that you haven't a penny to your name, I highly doubt she'll willingly hand it over to you free of charge."

"So let me get this straight," said Beau irritably. "Ezra gets the extra legroom, Aunt Christine gets to sit by herself, and I get to be stuck in a row full of girls." He shook his head despondently, "This is so not how I saw my vacation playing out."

"Well, technically she isn't sitting by herself, Beau,' said Mom. "She's having to sit in the middle seat just like you, except she has to sit between two people she doesn't even know, and that's not always an easy thing to do, believe me."

He slowly looked over his right shoulder and watched as Aunt Christine laughed and talked animatedly amongst her fellow seatmates, "Yeah, well, you might want to mention that to her."

As Beau continued to lament over his unfortunate seat assignment, Grandma Helen was finding herself having to wage a battle of her own (one-sided, of course), against the exposed feet of a rather large man sitting in the aisle across from her.

"Oh, dear God, that man's feet are absolutely repulsive!" she hissed. "I think I'm going to be sick."

"Shh, keep your voice down," whispered Mom. "There's no need to be ugly about it."

"The man's feet look like he could swoop down from the sky and snatch his dinner from a lake, I'm not being ugly, Olivia, I'm being candid," she explained. "And the fact that he has the audacity to wear flip-flops out in public is like adding insult to injury, so please excuse me for taking offense, I'm not used to seeing such vulgarity so openly displayed."

Mom leaned forward ever so slightly and scanned the floor next to Grandma Helen. She then drew back slowly and said, "Okay, I see what you mean, but the theatrics really need to stop." She opened her water bottle and quickly took a sip, "In fact, I think it would be best for all of us if you'd just avert your eyes altogether and not look at them."

"Don't look at them?" her voice went up an octave. "They're practically usurping the entire periphery of my left eye, Olivia, it's impossible not to look at them!"

"Well, there's not a whole lot you can do about it, Mother, so just stop obsessing over it, okay?" She opened her magazine to an earmarked page, "Besides, you're only going to make things worse for yourself and everyone else if you don't."

"That's easy for you to say, you're not the one who has to sit directly across from him in a confined space for the next ten hours," she sneered. "I may as well cut my losses now and pass on dinner because there's no way I'm going to be able to keep any food down with those hooked claws staring up at me throughout the entire meal service."

"Well, you may want to think about canceling breakfast too, then," smirked Mom. "Of course, considering how much you despise airplane food; I hardly think it'll be much of a sacrifice."

"Trade seats with me, Olivia, please," she implored.

"And have my dinner ruined by those things, no thank you," said Mom. "Besides, you pitched an absolute fit earlier about having to have the aisle seat, so stop complaining, you got exactly what you wanted."

"Yes, but that was before the hairy bird man decided to sit next to me." She made a show of placing her left hand up against her face and shuddered, "Ugh, I can just feel his nasty toes lurking and it's making me incredibly uncomfortable; I need to have a buffer between the two of us."

Mom took another sip from her water bottle, "Sorry, no can do."

Realizing that Mom had absolutely no plans to capitulate, she immediately set her sights on Beau, "Darling, wouldn't you rather sit here on the aisle instead of between your mother and sister?" she cooed. "I can only imagine how cramped you must be right now."

"And sit next to raptor claws over there?" he snickered, "Thanks, but no thanks."

Before Grandma Helen could come after me with her less than appealing offer, she immediately noticed a young couple standing a few rows ahead of us trying to console their newborn.

"Oh, dear God, please tell me that family's only pausing momentarily before heading to the very back of this plane," she scowled. "I don't think I have the mental capability to handle both a wailing baby and gnarled feet all in the same flight."

Mom looked up from her magazine to see the husband placing items in the overhead compartment, "Uh, it looks as though they're here to stay, so you may want to go ahead and prepare yourself."

"Why do people always insist on being so selfish?" she demanded. "Why don't they ever take the time to stop and think about the ways in which their actions inconvenience and affect others?"

"You can't possibly be serious right now," said Mom. "Don't you think that's a bit like the pot calling the kettle black?"

"I may be self-obsessed and somewhat self-serving, Olivia, but I would never be so inconsiderate as to bring an infant onto a 10-hour flight." She laid her head back against the headrest and closed her eyes, "I do have some sense of propriety, you know."

"Believe it or not, I actually agree with Grandma," said Beau. "Newborns are loud, messy, and require entirely too much work, if you ask me. 'Wah, I'm hungry, wah, my diaper needs changing, wah, I'm not getting what I want.' He popped a few gummy bears into his mouth, "The list of complaints is endless, really."

"Sounds a lot like you," I snickered.

"And how exactly would you know any of this, Beau?" asked Mom. "Is there something you're not telling me?"

"Oh, I had an affair back in '86," he deadpanned. "It's a decision that quite honestly still haunts me to this very day."

As the plane began to taxi onto the runway, the baby's piercing screams began to escalate, and everyone, other than Grandma Helen, was doing their best to disguise their irritation, but the incessant wailing was definitely beginning to take its toll.

"Oh, dear God, this is going to require copious amounts of alcohol; I just know it," said Grandma Helen, despondently squeezing the bridge of her nose.

"The alcoholic in you must be jumping for joy right about now, yes?" said Mom acerbically.

"I'm not an alcoholic, darling, I'm a spirits enthusiast," she smirked. "And since it seems to be a family trait, it would probably do you well to learn the difference."

"I'll certainly try to keep that in mind, Mother, thank you," said Mom.

Shortly after takeoff, the flight attendants began making the rounds with the beverage cart, much to the delight (and relief) of both Mom and Grandma Helen. The crying newborn had thankfully quieted down and everyone seemed to be at peace. As we made our way across the Atlantic, we found ourselves each happily engrossed in our own forms of entertainment. Beau and I were both intently watching a movie (me a romantic comedy, him an action film), Grandma Helen was busy playing *Project Makeover* on her iPad while doing her best to ignore the unsightly feet of the man sitting next to her, and Mom was finishing up an article in her women's magazine about the trials and tribulations of motherhood.

After coming to the end of the article, Mom closed her magazine and looked directly over at Beau and me with tears in her eyes, "I love you both so much, you know that right?"

Not quite knowing what was happening, we simultaneously pulled the headphones from our ears and said, "What?"

"I just really need the two of you to know how much I love you, that's all," she said, wiping an errant tear from her eye.

"Oh, we're doing this right now, are we?" said Beau, rolling his eyes.

"Don't be a jerk," I said, nudging him.

"It's just that the two of you are growing up so fast and I just want time to stop, you know?" She teared up again, "I would give anything to go back and relive those days when you were little; I would make sure to take the time to really appreciate each and every moment and hug both of you just a little bit tighter."

"Exactly how many glasses of wine have they served you?" asked Beau. "Should we be concerned?"

"I'm not drunk, Beau, I'm just reminiscing," said Mom.

"Mom, please don't be sad." I reached over and took hold of her hand, "Beau, Ezra, and I love you so much, and we will never be too far away from you, I promise."

Beau looked down uncomfortably at our clasped hands, "Uh, look, if this is going to escalate into some kind of cry session, I'd really like to step away."

Completely ignoring him, I continued with tears of my own, "You mean so much to me too, Mom, and I hope you know that I'll always be here for you; you're my best friend."

"Ugh, please tell me this is almost over," whined Beau.

"Thank you, baby," she sniffed. She released my hand and pointedly looked over at Beau, "And thank you for indulging me in letting me tell you how much I love you."

"You know, you really may want to stop reading those parenting magazines, Mom," said Beau. "I seriously think they mess with your head."

"Look, I know you may not understand any of this now, but the love a parent has for their child is completely altruistic and self-sacrificing. There is absolutely nothing more important to any parent than to see their child happy, healthy, and thriving, so much so, that they are willing to do whatever they can for them, even if that means giving up their life, both literally and figuratively." She smiled over at him, "And it's my prayer that you'll be fortunate enough to know that kind of love someday, Beau."

"Oh, I already know what it's like to be a parent," answered Beau earnestly. "I recently adopted some kids on my Skyrim game, and let me tell you, it's a thankless job. I'm honestly thinking about selling them back to the man I bought them from because they're way too much work and require way more attention than I'm willing to give."

"You really know how to make a mother proud, son," she snarked.

"Yeah, well, it's a gift," he smiled.

"Darling, if you're through with that magazine, I'd really like to borrow it," interjected Grandma Helen. "I think it may be of some use."

"Since when do you care about reading parenting magazines?" asked Mom skeptically.

"Oh, I have no intention of reading it, dear," she scoffed. "I was just hoping to prop it up so that I don't have to view that man's vulgar finger toes anymore."

CHAPTER EIGHT

Seven hours later we found ourselves in the Milano Centrale Railway Station patiently waiting for the train that would eventually take us to Varenna, a small town located on the eastern shore of Lake Como. We were currently standing in line to get coffee and pastries from a small food kiosk in the corner of the station when Beau took notice of an older woman who was standing on the opposite side of the glass partition separating us. The woman, who looked to be in her early sixties and about two-hundred pounds overweight, was wearing a large flamingo-inspired Mumu that was nearly bursting at the seams. Her flamboyantly pink spiked hair harmonized perfectly with the outfit, and that, along with her multiple tattoos and colorful piercings, literally made her look as if she had just stepped out of a two-year old's kaleidoscopic coloring page. The finishing touch, however, was her three-inch-long hot pink rhinestone-covered fingernails, a garish embellishment that not only accentuated, but amplified the already gaudy polychromatic ensemble.

"Hey Ezra, do you see that really fat woman standing over there in the bright pink flamingo tent dress?" he asked.

"You mean the one who looks like Rainbow Bright and Jabba the Hut had a baby?" he answered. "Yeah, she's hard to miss."

"Okay, both of you stop it right now, I've raised you better than that," reprimanded Mom. "There's no need to be nasty about someone you don't even know."

"Geez, lighten up, Mom, it was just a joke," said Ezra defensively.

"Okay, fine, we'll play nice," conceded Beau. He then leaned in conspiratorially, "Did you see how long her freaky fingernails are? I'm telling you; I think she could give Freddy Krueger a run for his money."

"Her nails are long, yes, Beau, but she in no way resembles Freddy Krueger; that's a horrible thing to say," said Mom.

"The woman looks like she has cutlery for fingers, Mom," he pressed. "The resemblance is there, believe me."

"And whose fingers are we talking about, dear?" asked Grandma Helen joining in on the conversation.

"That big fat woman…" he paused, noticing Mom's disapproving glare, and then corrected himself, "I mean, the portly and rather obese woman standing on the other side of the glass partition behind us," he said.

Grandma Helen turned around and gasped dramatically, but before she had a chance to audibly register her deprecatory thoughts, Mom issued her a stern warning, "Not one word, Mother."

"You know, I really hate it when you do that to me, Olivia," she snapped. "I'm not a child, I'm your mother, and I don't need you telling me what I can and cannot say."

"Yes, well, they tend to be one in the same most of the time, so I've learned to take precautions," said Mom.

Grandma Helen gestured over to where the woman was standing, "You can't possibly think that's tasteful; she looks like a Phyllis Diller Oompa Loompa for God's sake!"

"That may be true, but you could at least tone it down a bit," said Mom. "You're being rude and insensitive and I don't want her to overhear you."

"Rude and insensitive?" she reiterated irritably. "No, dear, what's rude and insensitive is that dreadful pelican-themed ensemble she's put together; it's practically hurting my retinas, it's so bad."

"Flamingo," corrected Mom.

"Whatever, it's still a bird," she dismissed. "The point is, it's an eyesore, and you and I both know it."

"Look, I'm just asking that you keep your voice down, that's all," soothed Mom. "It has a tendency to carry far and wide and I really don't want to have to deal with the repercussions of your loose tongue so soon after landing in a foreign country."

"That's a tad bit dramatic, dear, don't you think?" she scoffed. "But, if it will make you feel better, I will avert my eyes and say no more."

"Thank you, I would appreciate that," said Mom.

"So, how do you think she wipes her butt with those things?" wondered Beau aloud. "I mean, I've been turning it over and over in my head and I can't imagine how that's even possible."

"I would think that she uses a bidet," I answered.

"What's a bidet?" asked Beau.

"You'll be finding out soon enough," I laughed cryptically.

Noticing the look of confusion on Beau's face, Ezra chuckled softly, "It's basically a toilet that shoots water up your butt like a squirt gun making it so that you don't need to wipe."

"It shoots water up your butt?" he raised his brows. "That can't possibly be lawful."

"It sure does," I smiled devilishly. "And in a nice even stream too."

"Okay, well, that's both disturbing and incredibly intrusive," he said. He turned toward Mom, "Please tell me you've prepared accordingly for this."

"It's a European thing, Beau," said Mom. "But don't worry, the bathrooms will still have toilet paper for you to use."

"Wait, so you're telling me that people actually choose to sit on an invasive butt fountain when there's a perfectly good roll of toilet paper that can do the exact same job in less time?" he asked incredulously. "That's messed up."

"Like I said, it's a European thing" shrugged Mom.

After placing our order, we received our coffee and pastries and made our way over to two small round tables in the opposite corner of the kiosk. The placement of the tables allotted us an unobstructed view of the woman in the flamingo Mumu. I watched as she expertly pulled out a small vial of perfume from her purse, spritzing herself from head to toe and everywhere in between. The pungent and flowery perfume quickly made its way across the partition and over to where we were sitting, enveloping us in its effluvious scent.

"Oh dear God, what is that abhorrent stench?" sniffed Grandma Helen. "It's literally making my eyes water."

"Um, I think it may be coming from that lady's perfume, I just saw her take it out of her purse," I said.

Ezra looked up from his chocolate croissant and slowly shook his head, "I tell you, that's like adding insult to injury, right there."

Beau shrugged nonchalantly and opened his orange juice, "Well, it's kind of giving me slapping lipstick on a pig vibes, but hey, it is what it is."

***

Once we were seated on the train, we each settled in for the hour-long ride up to Varenna. Dad and Grandpa Anthony had pulled up a depth map of Lake Como on their phones and were discussing how it ranked amongst other lakes in the region, Ezra was texting nonstop with Sabrina, Beau was watching YouTube videos, Grandma Helen was editing recent pictures of herself, and Mom was having a lengthy Facetime call with Churchill, a feat made possible solely by the impertinent hijacking of Aunt Christine's phone while she was talking with Brian.

As for me, I did nothing but gaze out the window and greedily drink in the beauty that is Italy. The lake had just come into view, and to say that it was breathtaking would be an understatement. We have some lovely lakes in and around different parts of North Georgia, but nothing that compares to the majesty that is Lake Como. As the train made its way further north, I watched as the verdant flat countryside gave way to a more rugged mountainous one, its tall, towering peaks sheltering the lake within it, allowing it to nestle deep within the confines of its protection. The calm cerulean water glistened brightly with the reflection of the afternoon sun and everything looked peaceful and calm.

"Okay, bye-bye, Churchie," gushed Mom. "Mommy has to give the phone back to your Auntie but be sure to be a good boy for Uncle Brian and know that Mommy loves and misses you so much!" She handed the phone back to Aunt Christine, "Thank you for indulging me."

"As if I had any choice in the matter," said Aunt Christine sardonically.

"I'm sorry, I just miss him so much," sighed Mom. "I don't want him to worry and think that we've abandoned him or that we don't love him anymore."

"I think you're giving that dog entirely too much credit, but by all means, please keep commandeering my conversations to prove your love and adoration for him," she retorted sourly.

"Honestly, dear, you sound absolutely ridiculous talking to that animal like he's human," said Grandma Helen. "Other than his name, I highly doubt he has any clue as to what you're saying, so please stop making a fool of yourself."

"Oh, I see someone's forgotten to take their happy pills today," said Mom cheerily.

"It's probably more like she hasn't had enough wine and is going through withdrawals," snarked Aunt Christine.

Mom nudged Grandma Helen softly with her foot, "Hey, what's got you so grumpy?"

"I'm utterly exhausted," she said. "I couldn't sleep one wink on that plane and I think it's starting to catch up to me."

"Well, had you not batted away the neck pillow and sleep mask I brought for you, you might have found that you'd gotten a little sleep," said Mom. "The rest of us certainly did."

"Have you completely lost your mind, that would have messed up my hair and make-up!" she exclaimed. She reached into her purse, pulled out a compact, and began scrutinizing her lipstick, "I absolutely refuse to sleep in public, Olivia, you know this.

"Why won't you sleep in public, Grandma?" I asked, my interest piqued.

"Because everyone that does always looks dreadful, and I want absolutely no part of that," she said.

"So you're saying that you look better when you sleep privately?" asked Aunt Christine, her voice belying the question.

"No, that's not what I'm saying, Christine," she bristled. "What I'm saying is that you'll never see me looking anything but utterly fabulous whenever I'm out in the public eye."

"It's true," said Grandpa Anthony, chiming in on the conversation. "I remember a time not so long ago when your Mother accompanied me to Dallas for a culinary convention. The weather had taken a turn for the worse, putting our hotel under a tornado warning, and when she learned that it wouldn't be lifted until midnight or later, she refused to take off her make up or put on her pajamas for fear of who might see her if we had to leave the room to take cover."

"Oh, dear God, please tell me that's not a true story," said Mom.

"Hand to God, it's the absolute truth," he smirked amusedly.

"I'm sorry, but there was no way in hell I was about to enter into that corridor looking anything less than put together," said Grandma Helen. "And neither should anyone else."

"I hate to burst your bubble, Mom, but I can assure you that if a tornado were ever to hit, the very last thing on anyone's mind would be who you are, how you look, or what you're wearing," offered Aunt Christine pragmatically.

"I don't care," she shrugged, closing her compact. "I will never allow myself to look unsightly or dowdy, I'm not one of those Walmart people, you know."

"Yes, we are well aware of that, Mother, believe me," said Mom rolling her eyes.

"You know, I've been thinking," said Beau offhandedly.

"That would be a first," chuckled Ezra.

"Shut up, dork," he retaliated.

"Okay, that's enough," said Dad. He unscrewed the cap on his water bottle and took a swig, "What have you been thinking about, son?"

"I've been thinking about getting a Venus Fly Trap and naming it Taco," he said. "I've been wanting one for a long time, actually."

"You want a what?" interjected Mom incredulously.

"A Venus Flytrap," he answered earnestly. "It's a carnivorous plant that eats insects."

"I know what it is, Beau," she clarified. "I just never thought I'd have to bring one into my home."

"Okay, so hear me out," he said. "I've been watching this guy on YouTube that breeds them and he says that they can live up to twenty years, so I figure It might be a good starter pet for me." He turned his phone around to show a picture of the toothy-looking plant, "And since you won't let me get another dog, I'm thinking this might be a good alternative."

"Oh, dear God, that thing is absolutely hideous!" said Grandma Helen, curling her lip.

"Son, a Venus Flytrap is not a pet, it's a plant," said Dad pointedly.

"Actually, the guy I watch says that even though they're plants, they also make excellent pets because they produce very little waste and are pretty much self-sufficient as long as you provide them with plenty of water and bugs to eat." He turned the phone back around and added, "I've actually done a lot of research and would be more than happy to present a PowerPoint with my findings to both you and Mom once we get home."

Aunt Christine leaned over and quietly snickered in Mom's ear, "I bet you're rethinking all those research projects you made him do right about now, huh?"

"Ugh, I know," sighed Mom. "Why do I have to be so good at what I do?"

CHAPTER NINE

"What do you mean there are no taxis?" asked Grandma Helen. "Have we arrived in some third-world country I'm not aware of?"

The fact that she was posing this absurd question with the opulent and luxurious Lake Como serving as the backdrop to her query was not lost on any of us, especially Mom.

"Yes, Mother," said Mom, grandly gesturing to the lake view behind her. "We've decided to vacation in the Democratic Republic of the Congo. In fact, the hamlet that we'll be staying in is just down the way, and from what I understand, they've kindly prepared a smattering of cassava, legumes, and bushmeat in honor of our arrival." She adjusted the bag strap on her shoulder and then added, "I also took the liberty of packing a colorful Liputa dress in your luggage, so please be sure to wear that to dinner tonight, this way you'll be able to blend in with local culture and not look so foreign and out of place."

"I see," said Grandma Helen coolly. "Apparently I'm not the only one who forgot to take their happy pills today." She turned around to face the parking lot, "What I meant before I was so rudely ridiculed, is that it doesn't make any sense. Train stations are notorious breeding grounds for taxis, it's where they make their livelihood, I just find it odd that there aren't any around waiting for fares, that's all."

"Well, Varenna's a pretty small town, so there probably aren't many cabs to begin with," said Dad. "Plus, I think it's fairly common practice for most people to walk down to their accommodations rather than drive, especially considering the town center is less than a quarter of a mile away."

"A quarter of a mile?" she gasped. "Have you not seen all of my luggage?"

"Yes, master, Dobby has seen your luggage," chimed in Beau. "Perhaps master would be so kind as to toss Dobby an old sock so that he will no longer have to drag it all behind him."

"Okay, it's not like you're having to do it alone, you know," said Ezra. "Besides, I'm the one that got stuck with the really big bulky one."

"Yeah, well, at least you only have to deal with one," said Beau. He lifted the bag hanging from his shoulder, "I'm the one that's having to haul this enormous satchel of make-up and oversized carry-on wannabe in addition to everything else."

"Okay, both of you stop," warned Dad. "We're all in this together, I'm having to carry an extra bag too, so just suck it up, both of you."

"You know," said Grandma Helen, completely oblivious to the argument taking place behind her, "Now that I think about it, it may just be easier to call an Uber." She pulled out her phone and began scrolling through the app, "I just need to make sure we can get one large enough for all eight of us."

"You do realize we're in Italy, yes?" asked Aunt Christine. "The streets are narrow and the cars tend to be small and compact; our luggage alone wouldn't even fit in one."

"We'll just order three, then," she chirped happily. "Problem solved!"

"You know, honey, it's really not that far away," said Grandpa Anthony. "And, had we not been standing here lollygagging this entire time, we'd probably already be there by now."

I am not lollygagging, Anthony," she bristled. "I'm being practical."

"Is that what we're calling crazy these days?" muttered Ezra.

"Okay, look, I've got the apartment pulled up on the map," said Dad. He sidled up next to her and said, "Do you prefer reading maps in satellite view or map mode?"

"I generally try not to read maps at all, dear," she answered plainly.

"Okay, we'll just stay in map mode, then," he said, looking down at the screen. "If you'll notice, the map is showing that the apartment is less than a ten-minute walk away and mostly downhill, so we should be able to arrive at our location long before an Uber can even get here."

Grandma Helen desperately scanned the front of the train station for anything that would help her avoid having to make the brief walk into town.

"Don't you think with it being such a small area, that there would be some sort of alternate transportation around here like a pedicab or rickshaw?" she asked earnestly.

"A rickshaw?" exclaimed Aunt Christine. "You can't possibly be serious."

"Oh, dear God, this isn't 1870's Japan, Mother," said Mom. "What is wrong with you?"

"Okay, fine, I'll walk." She relented irritably. She set down her purse and crossed her arms accusingly, "Will you at least allow me to use the restroom before making me schlep all of my belongings into town like a pack mule?"

"What do you mean, 'schlep all of your belongings?'" snarked Beau. "Last time I checked, the only thing you had to worry about was your purse and sunglasses, it's Ezra, me, and Dad that..."

Mom calmly reached over Beau's shoulder and firmly placed her hand over his mouth, "We'll be waiting for you right here, Mom," she said.

"Thank you," she smiled primly.

We all watched as Grandma Helen slowly sauntered her way over to the small outlying building that served as the public restroom, and then we all watched as she briskly walked back out twenty seconds later.

"Wow, that was fast," said Mom.

"Yes, well, there isn't any toilet paper," she said in exasperation. "Of course, I really shouldn't be surprised with the way this day is going."

"Oh, here, use this," said Mom, pulling a small plastic baggie out of her purse. "I read that many of the public restrooms in Italy don't have toilet paper, so I made sure to come prepared." She handed her the roll of tissue, "This should at least make things a little bit better for you."

"There's no toilet seat either," she retorted sourly.

"Well, when in Rome... shrugged Mom happily, trying to make light of the situation.

"That is never going to happen, Olivia, I can assure you." She picked up her purse and haughtily adjusted her sunglasses, "Well, I suppose there's no sense in prolonging the inevitable, we may as well get this unpleasantness over with."

"Oh, come on, honey, think of it as an adventure," said Grandpa Anthony. "Lake Como is absolutely beautiful this time of year, it's not too hot, not too cold, not too overly crowded, it'll be perfect, you'll see. He grabbed hold of his luggage and gestured over toward Dad, "Okay, lead the way Kemosabe!"

Grandma Helen somberly fell into line behind Mom and Aunt Christine and quietly snarled, "God, I just want to slap him when he's peppy."

**

After a short and relatively easy walk into town, we arrived at our Airbnb, a Mediterranean-inspired building that was located less than a stone's throw away from the shore of stunning Lake Como. Situated directly above a popular local café, the spacious four-bedroom apartment was decorated in hues of varying blue, which immediately brought about a sense of tranquility that intertwined seamlessly with the serene beauty of the lake residing just outside its door. The hospitality manager, Gianni, a young man in his late twenties, had graciously agreed to meet us at the café and was now personally escorting us around the place that we would call home for the next three days. Upon completion of the tour, he casually walked into the kitchen, pulled out two bottles of Prosecco from the refrigerator, and placed them next to seven wine flutes that were sitting on the counter.

"Please accept this gift from all of us here at Vito Molo," he smiled radiantly. "The management and staff are thrilled to have all of you staying with us and we sincerely hope that your time in Varenna is both a memorable and relaxing one." He expertly popped open both corks and began pouring the wine, but before handing them out to us, he quickly made a detour back to the refrigerator and grabbed a bottle of sparkling water, which he proudly presented to Beau.

"For you, signore," he said, bowing his head slightly. "And hopefully, the next time you find yourself in Varenna, it will be wine, not water, that I serve you."

"Gee, thanks," said Beau, less than enthused. "Nothing like a chilled bottle of bubbly water to make you feel good about being left out."

"Darling, you are an absolute Godsend!" exclaimed Grandma Helen, greedily taking a glass of Prosecco off the counter. "That walk down from the train station was absolutely dreadful, so I'm sure you can imagine how desperate I am to drink that memory away."

"Oh no, signora, I am so sorry to hear that," he said, his face etched with concern. "Had you told me that you would be needing transportation, I would have been more than happy to make arrangements for you."

"Oh, so you do have taxis," she stated far too loudly.

"Taxis, personal cars, shuttle vans, anything you need, really," he said. "Would you like for me to arrange for a personal car to pick you up the morning you leave?"

"Yes, that would be very much appreciated, dear, thank you," she said.

"Of course, signora, consider it done," he nodded. He set the keys to the apartment down on the table, along with his business card, and then headed toward the door, "And please don't hesitate to call me if you need anything."

"Thank you so much, Gianni, you have been an absolute angel," gushed Grandma Helen. "I do so hope we'll be able to see you again before we leave."

"You'll almost always find me doing something around here, so I have no doubt that you will," he smiled warmly. He opened the door and then waved goodbye, "Arrivederci, my friends!"

The door hadn't even closed behind him before Grandma Helen squealed excitedly, "Is he not adorable?"

"Well, he's definitely not one to read the room, that's for sure," said Beau looking down despondently at his bottle of water. "I mean, what kid wants to drink bland bubbly water?"

"He's tall, handsome, well-mannered, and speaks perfect English," continued Grandma Helen. "He'd be absolutely ideal for you, Adelaide!"

"What?" I asked, practically choking on my Prosecco.

"Gianni, he's perfect for you!" she beamed.

"And about ten years too old, Grandma!" I exclaimed.

"Oh, don't let a little thing like age stop you, Addie," she said dismissively. "Back in my day I used to date boys that were much older than me, and if I'm being completely honest, I came to the realization rather quickly that a man with experience is much more capable than a boy with none, if you know what I mean."

"Ew," I shuddered. "Please stop."

"Balk all you want, my dear, but you'll eventually see that I'm right." She poured herself another glass of Prosecco, "Just ask your mother."

"Let's not and say we did," said Mom, sidling up next to me. She clinked her glass with mine, "So, how do you like the wine?"

"It's delicious," I said.

"Just be sure not to imbibe too much," she cautioned. "You don't want to make yourself sick or hungover."

"Well, it's not like I've never had a glass of wine before, Mom," I smiled. "You and Aunt Christine have included me in quite a few of your wine nights, remember?"

"Yes, I suppose we have," she chuckled softly. She then leaned in close and whispered, "You never want to drink on an empty stomach, always be sure to pace yourself, be sure to drink plenty of water, take two ibuprofen before bed, and watch out for your grandmother, she tends to be a wine hog."

"Yes, ma'am," I nodded obediently.

A few minutes later, while the rest of us were still getting acquainted with our new surroundings, Grandpa Anthony walked over to the double doors leading out to the balcony and pulled them open. The small, terraced area, with its colorful window boxes and Parisian-style table and chairs, was reminiscent of a picturesque postcard come to life, offering an enchanting panoramic view that not only encompassed the shimmering turquoise blue water but also proudly unveiled the many colorful multi-tiered villas and lush green Cypress trees encompassing the town. The highlight, however, at least for me, was the vibrant and radiant wisteria vines that enwreathed many of the villas and storefronts in bursting pink, purple, and white flowers, an addition that, in many ways, served as the perfect ornamentation to an already prismatic and bewitching hillside.

"Oh, Anthony, it's just exquisite!" exclaimed Grandma Helen. "I can't believe were finally here."

He gently placed his arms around her, pulling her close, "It's truly a magnificent sight to behold, isn't it?"

She sighed contentedly and leaned into his embrace, "Ti amo, amore mio."

"Anch'io ti amo," he said, returning her sentiment.

"A toast to Anthony and Helen," said Dad jubilantly, breaking up the quiet reverie. "Thank you so much for being dumb enough to allow all of us to accompany you on your trip to Italy!"

"Well, it just wouldn't be the same without you," laughed Grandpa Anthony. He then lifted his glass and said, "Salute!"

"Salute!" we all cheered in unison.

As the group happily enjoyed their wine, Beau unceremoniously plopped down on the couch and sarcastically yelled out, "Oh, don't mind me, or anything, I'll just be over here sipping from this exquisite bottle of sparkling water."

Chapter Ten

Our first full day in Varenna was a relaxing one and was spent lazily meandering the narrow-cobbled streets, hidden alcoves, and lakeside paths that make up the small, quaint, and relatively quiet hillside town. Over breakfast, we learned from a local couple seated next to us, that Varenna is considered to be one of the oldest and earliest settlements on Lake Como, its origins dating back to ancient Roman times, when a group of local fishermen discovered it around 769 AD. Since then, however, the once humble and unassuming fishing hub has grown into a popular tourist destination, its vibrant and colorful hotels, restaurants, and storefronts rivaling those found in Bellagio, a lavish resort town located directly to the south, where many celebrities and politicians have been known to stay.

After an hour of traversing the local landscape, Grandma Helen had finally had her fill of the outdoors and was beginning to drag slowly behind, gazing longingly as she did, at each of the local eateries and wine bars we passed by.

"You know, wouldn't it be nice if we could just sit awhile and enjoy this beautiful lakeside view?" she asked wistfully, pausing outside the door of a local bistro. "We're only here for three days, it seems like such a shame not taking full advantage of it while we can."

"Wait a minute, did she actually just say that she wanted to take some time and appreciate part of the natural world without being coerced?" asked Aunt Christine skeptically. "Okay, who are you and what have you done with our mother?"

"Chrissy's right," agreed Mom. "You hate the very essence of nature and anything outside of four walls, so what's really happening here?"

I do not hate nature, Olivia," she scoffed. "I just prefer that it stay outdoors and away from me, that's all." She then let out a deep sigh and decided to come clean, "Alright, fine, I'm tired, I'm bored, I'm hungry, I've had entirely too much outside time, and I'm ready for a drink." She crossed her arms in front of her, "There, are you happy?"

"You know, honey, just up the way is that swanky Hotel Villa Cipressi you've mentioned wanting to see," said Grandpa Anthony. "How about we go have a drink and maybe relax for a bit?"

"Oh, that would be absolutely wonderful, darling, thank you," she smiled warmly. Taking his hand, she allowed him to lead her to the front entrance of the hotel where, once through the ornate double glass doors separating them, she unceremoniously looked back over her shoulder at Mom and Aunt Christine and childishly stuck out her tongue.

"Wait, did she seriously just stick her tongue out at us?" asked Aunt Christine incredulously.

"I swear, having to deal with her is like dealing with a toddler," sighed Mom. "Except in her case, the cure for crankiness is a 64-ounce mimosa rather than a nap."

"Honestly, I'm surprised she even lasted this long," said Ezra. "I thought we were going to lose her once she finally realized we were heading in the opposite direction of the day spa."

"Well, at least we were able to get close to an hour out of her," I said optimistically. "That's certainly progress."

Dad sighed and gestured toward the front door of the hotel, "I suppose we should just go ahead and join them, then. It would seem that having to acknowledge and appreciate the complexities of the natural world in more time than it takes to eat a sandwich has taken its toll on your grandmother."

"Yeah, well, so does the abstention of all human emotion, yet that never seems to slow her down any," added Beau.

"Okay, very funny," said Mom, putting her arm around Beau. "Believe it or not, I do actually think your grandmother is trying; she knows how important this trip is to your grandfather and to all of us."

"I suppose you're right," he conceded. "I'm mean, she didn't even freak out once when the lake water kept splashing up behind us during that family photo this morning and considering the absolute meltdown she had when I accidentally squirted her with my Super Soaker Blaster last year, I'm pleasantly surprised to see her still out and about." He watched as she slowly made her way around the hotel foyer, "Of course, she did threaten to disinherit me if I ever did that again, but I suppose all's well that ends well right?"

"Your grandmother tends to have a flare for the dramatic, yes, but I know for a fact that she would never disinherit you," said Mom. "She loves you more than you know."

"Yeah, I know, I love her too," he smiled.

As the two of them made their way over to the hotel, Mom made sure to lean in close and say, "Nice use of the word abstention, by the way, that was quite impressive."

"Thank you," he said proudly. "I've been tinkering with my verbal arsenal a bit, and I really think it makes a nice addition, don't you?"

"Oh, most definitely," agreed Mom.

The Hotel Villa Cipressi definitely did not disappoint, and is an absolutely breathtaking display of wealth, grandeur, and opulence with its lavishly decorated interior, marbled Corinthian columns, intricately coffered ceilings, and stainless white alabaster floors. Considered to be one of the most beautiful and luxurious hotels in Varenna, this grand estate is known to offer some of the most amazing views of Lake Como, many of which have been featured throughout Instagram and all over TikTok. Originally built between the 15th and 19th centuries, this charming boutique hotel, with its tiered botanical gardens and soaring cypress trees, humbly serves as the perfect backdrop to the exquisite and imposing lake that lay just beyond its border.

While Grandma Helen and Grandpa Anthony were enjoying mimosas and crespelle, an Italian version of French crepes, under a shaded, vine-covered terrace, the rest of us decided to adventurously journey in and around the perfumed and enchanted gardens surrounding the estate. Upon entering the sumptuous and fragrant labyrinth of pathways, I was immediately enveloped in a maze of ethereal beauty that quickly called to mind many of the fairytale stories I would often read as a child. In fact, the whimsical story of Alice and her exciting adventures in Wonderland played over and over in my mind as I blindly followed along the mysterious botanical trail, its lavender-colored wisteria trees and tall pink myrtles playing a childish game of hide-and-seek with the beautiful lakeside view just beyond. As we ventured further along the winding path, we eventually came across a few ornate benches nestled deep within the alcoves of the century-old gardens, their stone facades beckoning visitors to take a seat and sit for a while.

"It is so incredibly beautiful and peaceful here," sighed Aunt Christine. "I really wish Brian was here to experience it with me."

"Has he ever been to Italy?" I asked, taking a seat next to her.

"No, he hasn't," she said. "He and his fiancée were planning to go for their honeymoon a few years back, but those plans were abandoned the minute the wedding was called off."

"Wait, Brian was engaged?" I raised my brows in surprise. "You've never told me that."

"It's not really common knowledge," she smiled wanly. "And it's also not something he broadcasts regularly either, so please don't share it with anyone."

"I won't, I promise," I said. "Does Mom know?"

"Oh, yeah, she knows, but no one else does," she answered. "Especially not your grandmother."

"What happened, if you don't mind my asking?" I said. "I mean, was it consensual?"

"Not really, no, or at least, not for his fiancée, it wasn't," she said, shaking her head. She pulled her feet up onto the bench and rested her chin on her knees, "Apparently, a close friend told him that she had been cheating on him with an ex-boyfriend whenever he traveled out of town for work, so as soon as he confronted her and learned the truth, he immediately broke off the engagement and asked her to move out."

"Oh my gosh, poor Brian," I gasped. "I can't believe that."

"And, from what I understand, it got pretty ugly afterward," she said. "She kind of went crazy and started spreading rumors around town that it was actually him that had been cheating and not her, which of course no one believed, and then, after realizing she had nowhere else to turn, she immediately moved in with the ex that she had been shacking up with, marrying him just a few months later." She looked over at me and smiled, "But, her loss is my gain, and as much as I hate that Brian was hurt in the process, I'm glad it happened, because it enabled him to eventually make his way to me."

"Wow, that sounds a lot like you and Jack," I said.

"I know, right?" she chuckled.

"Does it bother him that you've been talking to Jack recently?" I asked carefully.

"No, not at all," she shook her head emphatically. "He knows I would never take Jack back and is actually somewhat amused that he's trying to wiggle his way back into my life now that I'm happy and engaged." She laughed softly, "Jack's a dick, there's no doubt about it, but he was a big part of my life at one time, and Brian understands that."

We sat in silence for a while before I asked the question that had been nagging at me, "Why do you think people cheat, Aunt Christine? I mean, why do people feel the need to be with someone else when they've willingly already committed to another person?"

"Honestly, I'm not entirely sure," she sighed. "But, if I were to ponder a guess, it's probably because they're insecure in who they are and find it necessary to seek validation in anything outside of what they already have. They're disillusioned by their egos and are in constant need of an outsider's attention to make themselves feel worthy and complete."

"Dusty never really seemed insecure to me, but maybe I was only seeing what I wanted to see." I took in a deep breath and exhaled it out, "It doesn't really matter, anyway, I'm completely over him and have absolutely no desire to reconcile or even talk to him ever again."

"I think we've all been blinded by love at some point in our lives," she said somberly. "But the important thing is to always learn from your mistakes, and to take the embarrassment and hurt you felt, and look at it as a learning opportunity rather than an emotional attack." She put her arm around me and leaned in, "You'd be surprised how much you can learn about yourself, and what you're willing to put up with, when you stop being a victim and just acknowledge that the problem was never really you to begin with; it was just the deficiency and inadequacy that resided within the person that hurt you."

"That's exactly what Mom said," I smiled. "Maybe not word for word, but the sentiment is the same."

"Great minds, my friend," she chuckled.

"Great minds, indeed," I agreed.

As we continued to chat, we watched Mom make her way up from the water's edge to where we were sitting, "The view is absolutely breathtaking, isn't it?" she said.

"It's sublime," I answered amiably.

"I just received a text from Dad saying that Grandma and Grandpa want to take another family picture and that we all need to start making our way back." She slowly scanned the area for Beau, "Have you seen your brother anywhere, by the way?"

I was just about to tell her that I hadn't when he noisily ran up behind us, "Mom! I think I just encountered my first stalker," he exclaimed, slightly out of breath.

"What do you mean by stalker?" she asked with concern. "Where, when?"

"Down by the water," he pointed behind him. "There was this strange guy wearing some sort of squid hat or something, and he just kept staring at me."

"Oh, my God, Beau, why didn't you immediately come and find me?" she scolded.

"Because I wasn't worried and felt completely safe," he answered calmly.

"Honey, that's not something to ever take lightly!" she exclaimed. I've taught you better than that.

"Geez, he was just a kid, Mom, calm down," said Beau. "He was just some weird little kid wearing a rainbow squid hat that kept watching me, that's all."

Immediately on high alert, she asked suspiciously, "And what exactly is it that you were doing that made him watch you so intently?"

"Oh, I was running laps around all the trees down by the water pretending to be James Bond," he answered earnestly. He shook his head despondently and then added, "You know, this place is nice and all, but Monte Carlo, it is not."

Mom looked down at him and arched her brow accusingly, "And you're telling me the kid in the rainbow squid hat is weird?"

Chapter Eleven

"Ugh, I absolutely hate being herded like cattle," sneered Grandma Helen. She scanned the crowd of people surrounding us, "I mean, surely there must be some better way to formulate a line than this." She crossed her arms in front of her, "Honestly, I think we should've just rented a car when we had the chance and driven over to Bellagio, it certainly would have been a more pleasurable experience if we had." She irritably jostled herself away from a rather large woman standing behind her. "And at the very least, I wouldn't have to stand here and be manhandled by Helga the Hun."

"It's not that bad, Mom," said Aunt Christine. "And she's not manhandling you, so just stop with all the theatrics."

"You know, I think you may have your cultural references confused, there, Grandma," said Ezra.

"What in the world are you talking about, dear, what cultural references?" she asked exasperatedly.

"Well, the Huns were a nomadic people that originated in Central Asia, whereas the name Helga derives its roots from Scandinavian and German heritage, so when you stop to think about it, the two don't really go together if you know what I mean," he said.

"Thank you, Stephen Hawking for that insightful anthropological insight," she snarked. "My God, you're starting to sound more and more like your mother every day."

"Actually, Stephen Hawking wasn't an anthropologist, he was a…"

"Just stop while you're ahead, Ezra," Mom cut in. "It will only drive you crazy if you continue to play the game, believe me." Turning her attention over to Grandma Helen she said, "And as we discussed earlier, the ferry is the easiest, fastest, and most direct route over to Bellagio, so you're just going to have to suck it up and stop your complaining."

"Ugh, fine," she rolled her eyes.

"I'd also like to remind you that you were in complete agreement with this plan last night when Dad brought it up at dinner, or don't you remember?" asked Mom.

"I was full of wine, cheese, and merriment, Olivia, of course I don't remember," she answered defiantly.

"Okay, well, not only were you amenable to taking the ferry, but also ebulliently raised your glass in celebration of the fact that the covered deck would act as a natural deterrent to wind-tousled hair," said Mom pointedly. "So, maybe you should think about that the next time you decide to drink three bottles of wine in a four-hour period."

Last night, Grandpa Anthony surprised us all by announcing that he had secretly reserved a two-hour private boat tour of Lake Como for the following morning. The company, Bellagio Yacht, had been recommended by his friend, Carl, who had just recently returned from a family vacation a few months ago. Carl and his wife, Cindy, had raved about the experience and urged Grandpa Anthony to book a tour for all of us while we were here. With the company operating primarily out of Bellagio, there would have been a substantial cost to have the yacht come pick us up in Varenna, so, after weighing the options, he made an executive decision for us to go to them, and it was during last night's dinner that we unanimously decided the best option would be to take the ferry, a decision that my Grandmother has apparently forgotten."

"Well, thank you so much, Dr Phil, for those insightful words of wisdom," snarked Grandma Helen. "You can be sure I'll be mulling them over during the first sips of my daily morning mimosa."

"The boat is coming!" exclaimed the large woman standing behind Grandma Helen. "I can see the boat!"

"Oh, dear God, please don't be one of those people," groaned Grandma Helen.

The woman looked over at her husband who was carrying a small child in his arms.

"Do you see the boat, Abigail?" she asked excitedly. "Daddy, show her the boat!"

"Boat! Boat!" shouted Abigail excitedly. "I want to see boat!"

"There it is, sweetie," said the dad, lifting the girl up onto his shoulders.

"Yay!" cheered Abigail. "Boat! Boat!"

"Yay, the boat is coming!" rejoiced the mother.

"I see boat! I see boat!" continued Abigail.

"Are you ready to get on the boat with Mommy and Daddy?" asked the woman.

"Sweet Jesus, I'm certainly ready," said Grandma Helen, pinching the bridge of her nose, trying to block out the child's endless chants.

"Boat! Boat! Boat!" clapped Abigail enthusiastically. "I see boat!"

Grandma Helen leaned in close to Mom, "I'm telling you, Olivia, I don't know how much more of these people I can take."

"The ferry is almost here, so just try to stay calm, okay?" soothed Mom.

"That's easy for you to say, you don't have Tattoo and Mr. Roarke breathing down your neck," she hissed. "It feels like I've plummeted unceremoniously into some sort of *Fantasy Island*-themed hell, only rather than living out the fantasy, I'm stuck having to endure the never-ending nightmare of hearing, 'the boat, the boat' on endless replay."

For those of you unfamiliar with the popular and long-time-running TV show, *Fantasy Island*, please allow me a moment to briefly explain. Having originally aired in the late 1970s, the show's premise primarily centered around a luxurious tropical island resort and the wealthy guests who paid inordinate amounts of money to have their innermost fantasies fulfilled (and no, before you ask, they were not those kinds of fantasies). Anyway, each episode would begin with the resort manager, Mr. Roarke, and his sidekick, Tattoo, eagerly awaiting the local seaplane that would bring each week's guests over to the island. Once the plane was safely in sight, the 3'11,' Tattoo, would then excitedly ring the tower bell, point enthusiastically up in the air, and yell out in a French accent, "De Plane! De Plane!," thus announcing the arrival of their soon-to-be guests. It is this particular scene that Grandma Helen is referring to, and as much as I hate to admit it, she's right, the child is very much reminiscent of the quirky little French man, but rather than a miniature three-piece white suit, this young impersonator is proudly wearing a bright pink sparkly t-shirt that touts, "Kind of annoying, but cute!"

"Boat! Boat!" continued Abigail. "I see boat!"

Having finally reached her boiling point with both Abigail and her parents, Grandma Helen whipped her head around, practically staring daggers at all three of them, before expertly donning a spurious smile that completely belied her thundering outrage.

"Hello, Abigail," she then paused momentarily to address the parents, "It is Abigail, yes?"

"Yes, that's right," they nodded enthusiastically. "Abigail, can you say hello to the nice lady?"

"Hi," she said uninterestedly.

Feigning amiability, Grandma Helen cleared her throat and smiled, "Abigail, I want you to know that I find it quite impressive that you've been able to alert every single person within a ten-mile radius that the ferryboat is almost here, but rather than continue to boisterously scream aloud that fact, could you maybe dial it down a bit and perhaps whisper your celebratory chant rather than scream it directly into my right ear?"

"Oh, I'm so sorry," said the father. "She's just really excited about her first boat ride, that's all."

"We'll be sure to quiet her down," smiled the mother penitently. "Thank you for letting us know."

"Of course, dear," she smiled. Glancing up at the young girl still sitting atop her father's shoulders, she added, "Be sure to enjoy your trip, Abigail."

Mom immediately pulled Grandma Helen in close and hissed, "You really need to be nicer about things, Mother."

"I'm always nice; I was nothing but nice," she said innocently.

"I mean genuinely nice, not bitchy nice," said Mom. "There's a big difference."

"I said thank you, Olivia, and even gave the child a warm smile," she answered defensively. "What more do you want me to do?"

"I want you to start thinking about how your insincere expressions and disingenuous benignities affect others. I want you to understand that tearing people down just for the hell of it isn't always the answer." She paused momentarily and then added, "I want you to choose kindness over spite."

"Okay, well, you're kind of tying my hands, here, darling," she answered defensively. Noticing the crowd beginning to move, she immediately fell into step with them, "Okay, everyone, it's time to set sail; chop, chop!"

Aunt Christine leaned in close to Mom and said, "I swear, trying to make sense of that woman's behavior is like trying to smell the color nine, it's virtually impossible."

After a short and relatively uneventful ferry ride, we reached the town of Bellagio, where, in a manner of minutes, we were introduced to the glamorous and romantic city that is often referred to as "The Pearl of Lake Como." The narrow cobblestoned streets and alleyways were lined with a variety of colorful boutiques, each one boasting of high-end wares such as clothing, jewelry, and leather goods, while the enticing scent of warm pastries and freshly ground espresso from local bistros and coffee shops permeated the lakefront air. It was truly an idyllic setting, and had I been given the time, I would have been more than happy to lose myself in the maze of alleyways and paths that curved in and around this small yet magnanimous city.

Upon reaching the marina, we immediately met up with the skipper of the yacht, Luca, a seemingly good-natured man in his late thirties who had the kindest eyes I had ever seen.

"Buongiorno, my friends," he waved excitedly. "Welcome to Bellagio!"

"Buongiorno," we called out in unison.

"My name is Luca, and this," he gestured proudly to the beautiful 33-foot yacht looming behind him, "is Maria. We are both so happy to have you join us for a beautiful tour of Lake Como today." He casually rested his hands in the pockets of his windbreaker, "Tell me, have any of you been sailing before?"

"Nothing on this scale, no," answered Grandpa Anthony.

"No, I've never had the opportunity," said Dad. "In fact, I think this is a first for all of us."

"Well, then, I'm honored to be able to take you all on your first journey," he beamed happily. He quickly checked his watch for the time and then said, "Are there any questions before we get started?"

"I have one, dear," said Grandma Helen, holding up her hand.

"Yes, of course," he nodded at her.

"Do you happen to have any sparkling wine on board?" she asked.

"Are you serious, right now?" questioned Mom.

"Oh, don't tell me it never crossed your mind, Olivia," she scoffed.

"Yes, signora, we have more than enough," smiled Luca.

"I highly doubt that," mumbled Beau.

Grandma Helen held her hand up again, "I was also wondering if there might be a certain place for me to sit where I won't be affected by the wind, I don't want it to mess-up my hair and make-up."

Luca stared silently for a few seconds as if waiting for her to tell him that she was joking, but when she continued to look expectantly over at him, he immediately snapped out of his confused reverie and said, "Um, I suppose you can always go down into the cabin area if it gets to be too much, but the weather is quite mild today, signora, so it really shouldn't be much of a problem."

"Yes, well, let me be the judge of that, dear," she smiled sweetly.

"Okay, are there any other questions?" he asked.

"I don't think so," said Dad shaking his head.

"Excellent, let's get started, then." He turned to step onto the boat and then added, "Oh, and if everyone could please take off your shoes before coming aboard, that would be great."

"I'm sorry, what did he say?" asked Grandma Helen. "Did he just say we have to take off our shoes?"

"I'm pretty sure it's to keep the deck from wear and tear, Helen," said Dad, slipping off his shoes. "They probably make everyone do it."

As we began making our way onto the yacht, Grandma Helen pulled Mom over to the side and hissed, "I don't like to go barefoot, Olivia."

"You won't be barefoot, you have stockings on, remember?" asked Mom.

"And risk getting a run in them?" she shrieked. "No, absolutely not." She crossed her arms defiantly, "I'm not going."

"Oh, yes, you are," said Mom.

"Oh, no, I'm not," she stated stubbornly.

Mom lowered her voice and spoke in a hushed tone, "Now you listen to me, this boat tour is important to Dad, and since Dad is important to you, you are going to take off those shoes, step onto that boat, find a seat, and plaster a great big smile on your face, do you understand?"

Knowing deep down that Mom was right, Grandma Helen reluctantly began to take off her shoes. She then slowly shuffled her way over to the side of the yacht, her face contorting with each small step, and whined pitifully, "Ugh, I don't like this."

"It's a boat dock, Mother, not a carpet of roaches, so let's just get a move on, shall we?" said Mom, following closely behind.

"I'm doing what you asked, Oliva, now leave me alone to do it," she combated.

Grandpa Anthony watched proudly as Grandma Helen made her way onto the deck. He knew that she was completely outside of her comfort zone and the fact that she was willing to do this for him meant so much. As she continued to follow Luca over to her seat, she immediately glanced back at Mom and said, "There had better be a case of Prosecco on this damn thing."

CHAPTER TWELVE

It turns out there wasn't an actual case of Prosecco on board, although there was more than enough to appease Grandma Helen, as she not only enjoyed the Lake Como tour in its entirety but also raved continuously about the amazing time she had getting to know Luca. In reality, however, it was the other way around, minus the amazing part, that is. You see, Luca made the rookie mistake of showing an interest in Grandma Helen's foray into community theater, which then, of course, led to a one-sided discussion of the ins and outs of her entire theatrical career. So when I say that Grandma Helen enjoyed getting to know Luca, what I really mean to say is that Luca endured having to get to know her, and as we all know, that, in and of itself, can be an overwhelming and bewildering experience, and one I'm not so sure he'll soon get over.

After spending the morning packing and saying goodbye to Lake Como, we eventually hopped onto the train that would take us from Varenna down to Florence for the next leg of our journey. Grandma Helen, Aunt Christine, Mom, and Beau sat on one side of the train, while I sat directly across from them with Dad, Grandpa Anthony, and Ezra. We had just begun settling in for the ride when Grandma Helen pulled out a Bellagio Yacht pamphlet that Luca had given to her when we were leaving yesterday.

"You know, Luca was an absolute delight, I really enjoyed talking with him," she cooed. "In fact, I think I'll share this on my Facebook page and see if I can't help him drum up a little more business."

"You have four friends, Mother, and two of them are me and Christine," said Mom. "So I highly doubt he'll gain much traction from that."

"Oh, not my personal page, darling, my fan page," she congenially corrected.

"You have a fan page?" asked Mom confusedly. "When did that happen?"

"Beau helped me set one up a few months ago," she said. "We both thought it was high time I make myself more accessible to my fans."

"We?" he lifted his brow. "I'm pretty sure you were the one leading the charge on that one, Grandma."

Ignoring the slight, she continued, "Anyway, I've been sharing behind-the-scenes photos of the theater, funny memes, and personal experiences ever since; I've also been sharing some of our vacation photos with all of them, they're absolutely loving it!"

"You mean all six of them?" mumbled Beau, looking down at his phone.

Mom looked over at him disapprovingly, "Let's keep the sarcasm at a minimum, Beau."

"I actually have 23 people following me now, dear, with more and more joining every day," she touted proudly. "They are loving my content and I love feeling closer to my fans."

"If you say so," he shrugged nonchalantly.

Grandma Helen spread the pamphlet out on the tray table in front of her and snapped a few photos on her phone, "I'd really like to be able to help Luca, he expressed so much interest in me and my acting career, I just figure it's the least I can do."

"You literally had a captive audience, Grandma," muttered Beau. "It wasn't like he could jump ship or anything."

"Well, I'm sure he would appreciate that very much, Mother," said Mom, eyeing Beau warily. "In fact, you may even want to see if he has a business Facebook page so that you can tag him in the post, that way people will have direct access to his page and can contact him more easily."

"That's a brilliant idea, darling, thank you!" she exclaimed. She then cocked her head to the side as if she was thinking about something, "So, if I'm able to tag him in my post, will everyone that follows him be able to see who I am?"

"I believe so, yes," answered Mom.

"So then the people that follow him will see that Helen Vitali, Thespian is the one that tagged him, am I understanding that correctly?" she sought further clarification.

"Uh huh," nodded Mom absently.

"Oh, how wonderful!" she beamed jubilantly. "I may even find that I get more followers this way."

"Wait, what?" asked mom in confusion. "What name did you say you were using?"

"That would be Helen Vitali, Thespian," enunciated Beau slowly.

"Please tell me you did not allow her to use that name," whispered Mom.

"Well, I could, but I'd be lying," said Beau, casually scrolling through his phone. "Of course, the profile picture is what you should really be worried about, that's in an orbit all by itself."

Mom immediately tapped open the blue Facebook icon on her phone and typed in a search for Helen Vitali, Thespian.

"Why do you always insist on augmenting news you already know is bad, I wasn't even worried about her profile picture until now." She clicked on the name and quietly let out a breath, "Oh dear God, you can't possibly be serious."

The profile picture was a dramatized representation of Grandma Helen sitting on a stool in a black knit turtleneck and black slacks staring pensively up at a pair of hanging gold theater masks, her chin resting deliberately between her thumb and forefinger. At the bottom of the image was an overlayed personal quote that read, "Acting is the nutrient that feeds my soul – Helen Vitali."

"Told ya," snickered Beau.

"Yeah, well, I really wish you hadn't," said Mom. "I can't unsee any of this now."

"Hey, I told her it wasn't a good idea, but she insisted," said Beau.

Mom looked over at Grandma Helen who was still happily snapping photos of Luca's pamphlet.

"So, tell me, Mom, why exactly did you choose to use this photo for your profile picture and not something a little more upbeat; you look very somber and ruminative in this one."

"Oh, you found me!" exclaimed Grandma Helen. "Now you can follow me on that page too." She pointed to the profile picture displayed on Mom's phone, "Don't I look utterly fabulous? Everyone tells me that it's very reminiscent of Greta Garbo, so I simply had to use it."

"What does ruminative mean?" asked Beau.

"It means to think carefully, deeply, and deliberately about something," answered Mom. "It's also the complete antithesis of your grandmother."

"Are you saying that Grandma's shallow?" asked Beau.

"As shallow as a kiddie pool," said Mom.

"Okay, so I just posted the pictures on Facebook and gave him a glowing review, now all I have to do is sit back and see how many new followers I get," she smiled proudly. "This is going to be so much fun!"

"I don't think it really works that way, Mom," said Aunt Christine. She opened her phone to an incoming text, "Besides, I thought this was about helping Luca, not yourself."

"If I happen to get a little extra publicity from my charitable actions, darling, then so be it," she beamed brightly. "It's what I like to call good karma."

Mom noticed a slight smile come across Aunt Christine's lips as she responded to the incoming text.

"Hey, can you please tell Brian I'll Facetime him once I get to the hotel?" she asked. "I really miss Churchy and need to see his cute little face."

"Oh, this isn't Brian," she said.

"Who is it, then, dear?" asked Grandma Helen.

"It's Jack," she said looking up.

"What?" she shrieked. "Why in the world would you be texting with that vermin?"

"Mom, please stop," said Aunt Christine. "He's just telling me about a few places in Florence he thinks we might like to check out, that's all."

"Christine, that man is nothing but trouble," she warned. "He's trying to get back into your good graces, or maybe something else, I don't know, but you definitely need to stay away from him."

"It's fine, Mom, I promise," she said.

"And what about poor Brian?" asked Grandma Helen, crossing her arms sternly. "I can't imagine he'd approve of you texting back and forth with your meritless ex-husband."

"Brian knows that Jack and I are texting, Mother," she said calmly. "He also knows that I have absolutely no interest in him whatsoever and that as far as I'm concerned, we are strictly friends and nothing else." She opened a small bag of potato chips and offered one to anyone interested, "He also knows that Jack is well acquainted with certain parts of Italy, many of which we will be going to, and that he has also graciously made reservations for us at a few of his friend's restaurants, which having such a large party, makes it a lot easier."

"Yes, well, I certainly won't be eating there," she said defiantly.

"Mom, please, you have to understand that Jack and I are really just friends," she said imploringly. Taking a long inhale, she continued, "Listen, I held onto a lot of hate for a very long time, and I was absolutely miserable. Being with Brian has made me realize that I don't want to hold onto that hate anymore because in the end, it's just not worth it. Life is too short to be bitter and angry and I want to be free from all of that so that I can focus on a future with Brian; one that's filled with forgiveness and grace, not resentment and hate. I'm too old and too tired to hold on to grudges and grievances that do nothing but bring me pain; I'm ready to let go of that part of my life, Mom, so please let me try."

Grandma Helen sat in contemplative silence for a few moments and then shook her head solemnly, "I really hope you know what you're doing, Christine because you are playing with fire. That man has absolutely no soul and has never been interested in anything or anyone other than himself, you would do well to remember that."

"Yes, Mom, I understand," she nodded. "And I promise I'll be careful."

Two hours later, Mom, Grandma Helen, and I stood outside the Florence train station waiting for the others to go and get the rental car. The rental company was apparently located a few blocks away, and since nobody wanted to drag all of the luggage over there, the three of us opted to stay behind and wait for them to pick us up.

"I honestly don't understand how your sister can be so smart and so dense at the same time," said Grandma Helen. "I blame your father; he's always been so forgiving and benevolent."

"Well, I personally think it's a good thing," said Mom. "She's been harboring that hurt for a long time, I'm glad she's finally letting it go."

"Yeah, I really think she just wants to put it behind her, Grandma, that's all," I said.

"And as far as I know, Jack is only interested in friendship," added Mom. "He knows full well that she's marrying Brian and that she's very happy in that relationship, she's done nothing to make him think otherwise."

"I'm telling you, that man is not what he portrays himself to be, Olivia, he's up to something, I just know it," said Grandma Helen emphatically. "And with your sister being knee-deep in La-La Land right now, she isn't thinking straight and therefore can't see any of it for what it really is, which is deception."

"Look, she's an adult, you have to let her make her own decisions," said Mom. "As the mother of an adult child, myself, I completely understand how hard it is to let go, but Christine has been thriving ever since her divorce from Jack, and she needs to be supported right now, not ridiculed." She softened her voice, "You have to let her breathe, Mom."

"Okay, fine, you win," she conceded. "But if he does so much as one thing to make her fall into the trap I know he's setting, I will personally see to it that no one ever finds his body." She lifted her brow, "I have connections, you know."

"Yes, you've mentioned that on several occasions, Mother, and honestly I still haven't quite figured out whether or not you're joking," said Mom. "It's always been a bit disconcerting to me."

"Mom, I can assure you, she's just joking," I laughed.

"No, dear, I'm not," she answered stiffly.

"Oh," I said uncomfortably.

Just then a large silver Volkswagen passenger van pulled up directly in front of us, and before we had a chance to recognize who it was, the side-panel door slid open and Beau hopped out. He was wearing a cat that ate the canary grin as he yelled out excitedly, "Hey Mom, Dad already got cussed out in Italian for bad driving and it was so awesome!"

CHAPTER THIRTEEN

Once we were all settled in the van, Dad carefully maneuvered his way outside of Florence and into the suburbs of the surrounding region. The hotel we planned to stay in was specifically located in the Chianti region, a fairly sizable province of land that is considered to be the heart of Tuscany. Stretching primarily between the cities of Florence and Siena, Chianti's resplendent landscape is filled with thousands of dense vineyards as well as plenty of lush forests, medieval villages, and romantic castles. It is also considered the birthplace and namesake of the world's most famous red wine.

As we continued making our way in and around the flourishing Tuscan countryside, I found myself completely taken aback by the bewitching splendor that was literally sprawled out before me. The extensive panoramic landscape, with its verdant rolling hills and patchwork of vineyards, olive groves, sunflowers, and cypress trees continued on in unended succession as the prominence of the earthly terrain blended uninterruptedly into the colorful hues of the horizon. It was quintessential Tuscany at its finest, and it not only enraptured me but seamlessly rendered itself deep within my soul. It was truly a sight to behold, and had it not been for my family's constant back-and-forth-bickering, I would have happily continued to lose myself in the quiet reverie of its beauty.

"I'm literally in the back of the van, Mom, why can't I take my seatbelt off?" asked Beau.

"Because it will keep you from flying forward if something happens," said Mom. "You're father's driving like he's Mario Andretti up there and could quite possibly get us all killed, so I'm not taking any chances."

"I've forgotten how much I love driving a manual transmission," exclaimed Dad. "Hugging these tight curves is fun!"

"You know, dear, I'd really like to finish our entire vacation before I die if you don't mind," said Grandma Helen.

"And I'd really like to see Brian again," added Aunt Christine, bracing herself for impact.

"Hey, is anyone else hungry?" asked Ezra. "We've only passed like two restaurants in the past fifteen minutes and I'm starting to get a little concerned that there's nothing else out here."

"Okay Mom, listen," continued Beau. "If we get in an accident, you can just stretch your arm out like you normally do. It's the typical mom-stop, and since you have it down pat, I know my life will be in good hands."

"Stop complaining and just wear the damn seatbelt, Beau," said Mom. "And I do not have that down pat, I rarely ever slam on the breaks, that's your father's domain."

"Alright, I need everyone to stop whining about my driving," said Dad. "As I recall, I'm the only one in this family who knows how to drive a manual transmission, so unless one of you wants to take over, I suggest you just sit back and enjoy the ride."

"I don't get it," continued Beau. "A garbage man can literally hang off the back of a truck doing 40 mph, but I can't take my seatbelt off for one minute to find something in my bag, this is so unfair!"

"Don't be ridiculous, that argument has absolutely no bearing here and you know it," dismissed Mom. "A trash man can make his own decisions, you are still a child and cannot, it's as simple as that."

Oh, so you're saying that if I was a trashman you'd be perfectly fine with me taking off my seatbelt, is that correct?" he asked.

"No, that's not what I'm saying," she shook her head. "You know what, I'm finished with this conversation, you will continue to wear your seatbelt and that is the end of it."

"Seriously, I'm really hungry," said Ezra.

"And I need a drink," said Grandma Helen. "Darling, we are in desperate need of a winery, do you think you can make that happen?"

"Wouldn't you rather check in to the hotel and unpack first?" I asked.

"Do you really want to have to sit here and watch your mother continue to come unglued, Adelaide?" she raised a brow. "I know I don't."

"Anthony, would you mind pulling up the app we downloaded with all of the local wineries, please," said Dad. "I know we're getting fairly close to the hotel, but I think there may be one just up the way if I'm not mistaken."

Grandpa Anthony opened his phone and pulled up the map with all the local wineries, "Yes, there's a winery about 10 minutes from here, you even have it marked." He turned around in his seat and smiled at Ezra, "And it looks like they serve food."

"Sweet!" exclaimed Ezra.

Ten minutes later we found ourselves driving down a secluded gravel road with rows upon rows of flourishing grapevines flanking both sides. As we continued down the path, it eventually led us to a gravel parking lot where a quaint one-story Tuscan villa stood, its stone façade decoratively covered in thick viridescent ivy. To the left of the building was a 6-foot-tall rust-colored statue of a rooster with two large wine barrels on either side. Atop the barrels sat five wine bottles, a large bowl-shaped planter filled with various colorful plants and flowers, and a black and white sign that read "Daily Wine Tastings." On the other side of the building stood a tall white slab of vertically erect marble, decorated in whimsical wine-themed ornaments and metal-made letters that formed the name, Cantalucci. Directly to the side of that was a sizable wooden pen that had two black roosters happily pecking in and around a feeder trough.

"Mom, check out the roosters!" pointed Beau excitedly.

"Buongiorno!" came a voice from behind the pen. "Welcome to Cantalucci Vineyards." The voice belonged to an older gentleman dressed in jeans and a navy-blue button-down shirt, "I see you've met Giovanni and Leonardo."

"Yes, hello," waved Dad. "We actually just noticed them when we came to the door."

"Those two are usually up to no good," he laughed. "But since it is feeding time, you'll see that they are on their best behavior." He held out his hand to introduce himself, "My name is Alfredo Cantalucci, have you come for a tasting?"

"Yes, we have," answered Dad. "I hope this is a good time."

"It's always a good time for wine, my friend," he beamed. "Follow me, I have a table inside that will be perfect for all of you."

We followed Alfredo through the front door and over to a large round wooden table that was set up with multiple place settings, each with five wine glasses lined up in a row. He gestured for us to take a seat and then introduced a young woman who had just walked up beside him.

"This is my granddaughter, Gabriella," he smiled. "She will be helping me with the tasting this afternoon."

"Buongiorno," she smiled. "Would any of you care for something to eat? We have a wonderful selection of local meats and cheeses if you're interested."

"Yes, please!" Ezra yelled out. "I'm starving."

"Oh, okay," she laughed. "Well then, while my Nonno sets up the wine, I'll go and prepare a platter for you."

As Gabriella made her way back to the kitchen, Grandma Helen looked slowly around the simple, yet rustic room, "This is absolutely adorable, isn't it?" she cooed. "Very quant and farmhouse chic."

"Since when do you like anything farmhouse, Helen?" asked Dad skeptically. "You hate anything with this kind of motif back at home."

"Darling, I am about to drink delicious Italian wine deep within the hills of the gorgeous Tuscan countryside, not sitting down for a plate of ribs at The Saucy Swine with rusty farm décor and paper napkins," she admonished. "There's a substantial difference, you know."

"Hey, I like The Saucy Swine," said Beau. "It has a lot of character."

"Yeah, and all-you-can-eat pulled pork every Wednesday," added Ezra.

"And I'll have you know that their banana pudding has won numerous awards throughout the country," continued Beau. "Most BBQ restaurants can't claim that."

While Beau and Ezra continued to lament over Grandma Helen's disapproval of the Saucy Swine, Alfredo carefully wheeled over a cart with five different bottles and then placed them on the table.

"Will everyone be tasting the wine this afternoon?" he asked, lifting his brows.

"None for me Alfredo," waved off Beau. "I'm still trying to recover from the other night; I didn't really pace myself and drank way too much if you know what I mean."

Alfredo stared uncertainly at Beau, "Umm…"

"He's just kidding, Alfredo," smiled Dad. "He'll just have some sparkling water, if you have it."

"And could you maybe add some vodka?" asked Beau. "A little hair of the dog might be just what I need."

"That's enough, Beau," said Mom. "We don't need anyone thinking we're contributing to a minor in a foreign country."

"Ah, I see we have a jokester among us," he laughed. "You must really keep everyone on their toes, yes?"

"You have no idea," sighed Mom.

Alfredo lifted up one of the bottles and pointed to the rooster emblem on its neck, "Are any of you familiar with this particular logo?"

"No," we shook our heads.

"Well, the black rooster, like the one you see on this bottle, makes it possible to distinguish wine that has been produced within the Chianti Classico territory from those that have not, and since true Chianti Classico wine is considered to be a Denominazione di Origine Controllata e Garantita, or DOCG for short, any wine using this emblem must be taste-tested and approved by the Italian government before it can ever be bottled and sealed with this particular logo."

"So, what does that long Italian word mean, exactly?" I asked.

"It means that the denomination of origin has been inspected and guaranteed," answered Grandpa Anthony. "That it's been approved."

"Oh, you speak Italian?" asked Alfredo.

"I do," smiled Grandpa Anthony. "My parents were from Sicily."

"Oh, which part?" he asked curiously.

"Palermo, but they immigrated to the States before I was born," he answered.

"My family and I love to go down there and visit Cefalu, whenever we get the chance," said Alfredo. "It is so beautiful and peaceful there."

"Yes, it is, but I think Tuscany is even more beautiful," said Grandpa Anthony, raising his glass.

"So, wait a minute, you're telling me that someone actually has my dream job of tasting wine for a living?" asked Aunt Christine. "I seriously need to look into a career change."

"Not a bad way to spend your weekdays, no?" laughed Alfredo.

He poured a small amount of wine into everyone's glass, "The Chianti Classic Wine Consortium is an association of winemakers here in Tuscany that work to ensure the integrity of the Chianti Classico vinification process, and they do this by making sure that certain rules and regulations are met to authenticate true Chianti Classico wine. So, whenever you see this black rooster on the foil topper of your wine, you'll know that it is not only an authentic bottle of Chianti Classico, but it's also a wine that has been perfected over the years by generations of Tuscan vintners who have chosen to carry on the tradition."

As Alfredo finished talking, Gabriella walked up and placed a tray of assorted meats, cheeses, olives, and warm baked bread onto the table, "We have plenty more, so please don't be shy," she smiled.

"Bless you," said Ezra greedily filling his plate.

"Please, taste the wine and tell me what you think," encouraged Alfredo.

I picked up my wine glass and swirled the wine around carefully like Mom had shown me, allowing the aromas to evaporate out of the glass so that I could detect the various notes of flavor. I know this might seem a bit surprising, given my age, but my mother has done well to teach both Ezra and me the finer points of wine drinking, especially the one about always holding your wine glass by the stem so as not to look like, and I'm quoting here, "an uncivilized neanderthal heathen."

"Hmm, I think I smell berries with a hint of earthiness," said Mom. "Does that sound about right?"

"Yes, that is very typical of a good chianti," said Alfredo.

"You mean it smells like dirt?" asked Beau.

"No, but you can definitely smell the earthy and rustic aromas," she said. "Would you like to try?"

"Sure," shrugged Beau. He held the stem of the glass between his thumb and fingers just like Mom had shown him and lightly sniffed, "I just smell wine, Mom."

"Close your eyes and inhale deeply," she encouraged him. "You may find that you start to pick up notes of red cherry, leather, and certain spices."

"You know you kind of sound like one of those spiritual, not-for-Jesus people," he snarked. "I think I'll just stick with my water, thanks."

"So, exactly how is it that the rooster got chosen as the emblem and not something else?" asked Ezra.

"Well, it's actually a very interesting story," smiled Alfredo. "You see, for hundreds of years Florence and Siena fought mercilessly in the fight for unclaimed land, with mass casualties and tremendous bloodshed suffered on both sides. Eventually, each kingdom grew tired of the feud and agreed to create a permanent border between the two regions by having their knights ride out toward each other starting early in the morning, and wherever they met, that would then become the line of demarcation. And, seeing that there was no better alarm clock than a rooster back then, each kingdom carefully chose their own rooster to help with the situation. The kingdom of Siena chose a white rooster to wake up their knight while the kingdom of Florence chose a black one."

He carefully poured wine from a different bottle into a second glass and continued, "Now, here is where the story really gets interesting. You see, Siena made the grave mistake of feeding their rooster a hearty meal the night before, which allowed it a peaceful night of rest until daybreak when it awoke and alerted the knight that it was time to leave. Florence, on the other hand, didn't feed their rooster for days which made the bird hungry, restless, and squawking for hours. This then allowed the Florentine knight to get an earlier start, which enabled him to cover more distance, claim more land, and essentially earn the kingdom of Florence a massive piece of territory. So, as a sign of respect, Florence decided to make the rooster it's forever mascot, and that is why we use it as a label to authenticate true Chianti Classico wine."

"Wow, that's so interesting," said Mom. "I never would have guessed that was the reason behind all of this."

"Yeah, that is actually pretty cool," said Ezra, reaching for another plate of food.

"What a fun little story!" exclaimed Grandma Helen.

Beau leaned in close to Mom, "You know, I really think we should tell Alfredo to just lead with that story from now on and forget all of that DOCG sentimentalism, I was bored after the first ten seconds of his opening."

Chapter Fourteen

"I don't understand, the weather is absolutely beautiful," said Mom. "There isn't a cloud in the sky, why in the world would they cancel?"

"I think we got screwed," said Ezra. "Are you sure this was a reputable company, Grandpa?"

"Yes, they came highly recommended," he answered. "Unfortunately, Italians tend to do things a little bit differently than they do back home, so it's really not all that surprising."

"I still can't believe I was up at 3:45 this morning doing my hair and make-up only for them to cancel at the last minute," grumbled Grandma Helen. "I definitely plan on writing them a scathing letter, this is completely unacceptable."

"This was honestly the only thing I was looking forward to doing while we were in Tuscany," said Beau. "Now I'll probably just end up sitting through more wine tastings and boring history lessons, this bites."

"Ugh, this morning had been so full of promise," whined Aunt Christine. "I can't believe they canceled on us."

Aunt Christine was right, this morning had been full of promise. Grandpa Anthony had surprised us with yet another adventure, only this time it was going to be in a hot air balloon ride that would take us high above the entire Chianti region at sunrise. We were even supposed to land in a field of sunflowers and have a traditional Italian picnic breakfast with the pilot immediately afterward, but no, those plans had now been thwarted, and we currently found ourselves unceremoniously grounded, extremely irritated, and impatiently waiting for the hotel breakfast buffet to open. You see, rather than inform us of the cancellation last night, the balloon company decided it was best to wait until after we made the hour-long drive to the launching point (at the crack of dawn I might add) before texting Grandpa Anthony about rescheduling for the following day. They gave us no reason as to why they were canceling, and since we have plans to visit Florence and Montepulciano over the next two days, there's no way for us to reschedule.

"Listen, I understand that all of you are upset, and rightfully so, but I think I may have found an alternative that will appeal to everyone," said Dad. He held up his phone so that we could all see the screen, "This is Brolio Castle and is actually something we had discussed visiting at one point, and since it seems that we have a large pocket of time to fill now, I say we go and check it out."

"Wouldn't you rather spend the day winery hopping, dear?" asked Grandma Helen. "Sampling fine Italian wine around the Tuscan countryside sounds so much more pleasant than trudging around the prodigious grounds of a dark, dank castle, don't you think?"

"I'm with Dad on this one," said Ezra.

"Yeah, me too," agreed Beau. "Not to mention I've had my fill of sparkling water, thank you very much."

"You know, honey, there will be plenty of time to drink wine," said Grandpa Anthony. "And personally, I think seeing the local culture and history will be good for you, it may even help broaden your horizons some."

"But Anthony, we're in Tuscany!" she exclaimed. "This is literally wine country, it's what people come here to do."

Dad watched as the kitchen staff went to work setting out various tarts, meats, cheeses, and other breakfast foods before carefully adding his two cents.

"You know, Tuscany isn't just known for their wineries, Helen, it's also very rich in history with varying points of interest," he said. "And personally, I think we'd be doing ourselves an incredible disservice if we only focused on the wineries and nothing else; there's just so much to see and do here, and I'd really hate for us to miss it."

"Yeah, exactly," agreed Ezra. "Plus, it may not be a bad idea to take a break from all the wine and maybe add a little more clear fluid and rehydration back into our systems."

"Amateur," snorted Beau.

"Darling, it's important to stay hydrated, yes, but that doesn't mean you discontinue savoring good wine," said Grandma Helen. "We're literally surrounded by thousands of winemakers; it would be a disservice not to take advantage of that fact if you ask me."

"Apparently it's important to stay hydrated, but not necessarily sober," sing-songed Beau sarcastically.

"Stop," I nudged him.

"Okay, well, why don't we take a vote?" asked Grandpa Anthony. He raised his hand, "All in favor of checking out Brolio Castle for the afternoon, say aye."

"Aye!" we all raised our hands collectively.

Realizing she was in the minority, Grandma Helen sullenly crossed her arms over her chest, leaned back, and irritably let out a breath, "Okay, fine, Brolio castle it is."

With the breakfast buffet finally open, Beau and Ezra quickly jolted out of their seats and immediately began piling food onto their plates while the rest of us slowly got up to peruse the recently laid-out offerings.

"Hey, I know you're disappointed about all of this but you have to understand that not everyone wants to spend an entire day at a winery," said Mom, gently putting her arm around Grandma Helen. "You, me, and Christine, yes, but I think everyone else would really rather see some other sights, especially Dad and Greg, you know how much they love anything that has to do with history."

"Ugh, I know," she sighed. "They're both so boring,"

"Just do your best to try and stay positive about it, okay?" she said. "You may just find it's not as bad as you think."

"Yes, but touring a castle is going to take so much time, and since I have absolutely no interest in seeing it, I'd really rather not have to," she pouted.

"Well, think of it this way, you'll have a ton of interesting photos you can brag to your friends about once we get back home," said Mom. "In fact, you may even find that you want to share some of them with your followers on Facebook and give them a little more insight into the things you're doing. You know, just seeing pictures of you at wineries all the time can get a bit repetitive, but a medieval castle, now that'll really capture people's interest."

"Oh my God, Olivia, you're right," she said, letting Mom's words sink in. "This is the perfect opportunity for me to show my fans how diverse my interests are, and that I'm not only an artist, but also a scholar."

"Wait, what?" asked Mom. "That's not at all what I was trying to say."

Grandma Helen jumped up euphorically, "Oh, darling, this is wonderful! Everyone will be able to see that I'm not only talented but also a versatile and well-rounded individual to boot. They'll see that acting is simply something that I do, not necessarily who I am."

"But it is who you are," said Mom. "You told everyone on Facebook that acting is the nutrient that feeds your soul, remember?"

"Oh, that was just a little blurb for my Facebook page, I can change that any time," she dismissed, waving her hand. "Being forced into an afternoon of historical drudgery has made me see that I now need to show my fans that I'm more than just a serious stage actress; that I'm also a bit of a Renaissance woman with innumerable interests, talents, and hobbies."

"So, you're going to lie to them?" asked Mom.

"No, I'm not going to lie to them," she snapped. "I'm going to do exactly what your father told me to do, I'm going to broaden my horizons, deepen my interests, and take my fans along with me while I do it."

"Hey, Helen, it would seem you're in luck," called out Dad from the buffet table. "I just found out that Brolio Castle also has an award-winning winery, so you'll be able to obliterate yourself and learn something all at the same time, it's a win-win situation for all of us!"

"Oh, thank God," she said, picking up her plate and heading toward the buffet, "Because there was no way in hell I was going to be able to traipse around that thing sober."

"Hey, Mom," said Beau setting his plate down next to her. "Do you think Grandma has a drinking problem?"

"No, honey, Grandma doesn't have a drinking problem," she chuckled. "What in the world would make you ask something like that?"

"Well, it just seems like the only thing she cares about doing on this vacation is going to wineries and drinking wine," he said. "And since she does make up 25% of my DNA, I figure I should probably know what I'm in for when I grow up."

"Oh, honey, you have absolutely nothing to worry about," smiled Mom. "You just have to understand that Tuscany is kind of like your

Grandmother's Disneyland, so asking her not to go to wineries for a day is pretty much like asking a young child to leave the park before it closes, they're not going to be happy about it and will most likely throw a tantrum."

"Yeah, but I don't see you and Aunt Christine acting like that," he said. "And I know how much the two of you love wine."

"Yes, well, your Aunt and I are grown-ups," she winked. "Your grandmother, on the other hand, well, she's still trying to reach that stage."

***

Three hours later we found ourselves standing outside the rental van waiting for Grandma Helen to make her exit so that we could finally enter the castle grounds.

"We seriously could have toured the castle by now," exclaimed Ezra. "How much preparation does that woman need?"

"She's planning on documenting the entire visit on Facebook, Ezra, so we should probably just give her a little more time to get ready," I said. "She wants to look good."

"For 23 people?" asked Beau. "That's insane."

"You know, why don't we go and check out the gift shop while we wait," said Grandpa Anthony. "We can probably go ahead and buy our tickets there too and have them at the ready."

Just as we were about to turn and leave, Grandma Helen slowly slid the door of the van open and regally stepped out.

"Okay, now I'm going to need you to make sure and tell me if there isn't enough light while we film, Olivia." She then handed a small compact bag over to me, "And I'm going to need you to be a dear, Adelaide, and hold onto this while we film, I may find that I need to touch up my makeup while we're strolling about."

"Again?" asked Beau incredulously. "You literally just spent the last fifteen minutes in the car doing just that."

"Okay, now wait a minute," said Mom. "When I said I'd help, I meant that I would be willing to take a few videos for you, not direct an entire feature film; Martin Scorsese, I am not."

"Yes, well, we'll see about that, dear," she smiled primly. "Now, does this place have some sort of office where I can read over pamphlets and things of that nature in order to get a better understanding of this fortress thingy?"

That would be Brolio Castle, dear," said Grandpa Anthony. "And there's a gift shop just up the way that will probably have some information for you."

"Ooh, shopping!" she squealed in delight. "You know, this may not be as unpleasant as I first thought."

Brolio Castle is truly a magnificent sight to behold. It is one of the most impressive defensive castles in the Chianti region with origins dating back to the Middle Ages. Perched high atop a lone hill, it is but one of many in a network of imposing castles that were used to protect and defend the people living within the Gaiole region. Throughout the centuries, the castle has withstood numerous battles including those from the Aragonese and Spanish in the fifteenth century all the way up to the aerial bombings and artillery rounds that occurred during the Second World War. The fortress has been rebuilt and modified several times over the years and still proudly bears many of the scars it incurred through its various wars and battles. The castle eventually made its way into the hands of the Riscolli family in 1141 and is now considered to be the most extensive plot of land found in the Chianti Classico region, making up 1200 hectares with 240 of them serving as vineyards and 26 of them serving as olive groves.

Once we made our way through the castle gate we all decided to separate, with Beau and Ezra running directly up to the towers, Dad and Grandpa Anthony wandering over to the private chapel and family crypt, and Aunt Christine and I opting to stay with Mom, more for the sake of her sanity than anything else, as she obediently followed Grandma Helen around the luxuriant grounds.

"Mom! Mom!" waved Beau from the tower above, "They have arrowslits in the wall and I have Grandma in my sights, I could totally kill her if I wanted to!"

"What?" shrieked Grandma Helen. "What did he just say?"

"Calm down Mom, he's just excited, that's all," soothed Mom. "You can't take it personally."

"My grandson literally just yelled out to the world that he could kill me from a tower, how am I not supposed to take that personally?" she asked pointedly.

"Well, just be thankful he doesn't have a quiver full of arrows, Mom," said Aunt Christine. "I'm sure that kind of temptation would be hard to quell."

Seeing a look of horror pass over Grandma Helen's face, she quickly amended her last statement, "I'm just kidding, of course."

As the four of us continued to traverse the castle grounds, Aunt Christine and I made sure to stay back a good distance so that Mom could film Grandma Helen without any distractions. We had just walked up to a wall overlooking a vast expanse of land when Grandma Helen pulled out her pamphlet and began reading. A few minutes later, she put the pamphlet away, looked over at Mom, and told her to start filming.

"I need you to yell action when you're ready, dear," she smiled.

"You can't possibly be serious," said Mom. "Just start when you're ready."

"Would you please just yell action, Olivia?" she asked irritably. "I need to know so that I'm able to start on time."

"If that will make you happy, fine," she said.

"Well, I'm waiting," said Grandma Helen expectantly.

"Action," said Mom rolling her eyes.

Almost immediately after hearing the word, Grandma Helen completely transformed herself into the antithesis of who we know her to be and actually began to speak intelligently about the castle and its history.

"Brolio Castle, as you can see, is an exceptional representation of Medieval magnificence, but please know that it is definitely not without its scars." Grandma Helen patted the stone wall behind her and then looked back up into the camera, "Over the centuries, this magnificent fortress has been besieged and destroyed many times, with the last attack taking place during World War II. In fact, the damage from that war was so prominent that you can still see the shrapnel holes that now scar the entire stone façade covering this Italian monolithic stronghold."

As Grandma Helen continued to smile at the camera, she quietly continued saying the word "cut" over and over until Mom finally heard her and stopped filming.

"I honestly don't think I can handle much more of this," said Mom. "I really think it's time we just mosey our way down to the winery and put all of this ridiculousness behind us."

"Do you even think she has a clue as to what she's talking about?" asked Aunt Christine. "I mean, she actually sounded somewhat knowledgeable, but I know she's not."

Mom opened a pamphlet and pointed at a long paragraph, "No, she hasn't a clue, she just knows how to remember lines."

"That's still pretty impressive," she said.

"Can Grandma get in trouble for plagiarizing?" I asked.

"I highly doubt the 23 people following her will even know, honey," said Mom. "And since I really don't feel like lecturing her on paraphrasing protocols, I'm more than happy to let her take her chances."

"You know, I think we should go back over to the garden and do a retake; I really don't think I did a very good job authenticating myself," said Grandma Helen walking over to us.

"Actually, I think I have a better idea," said Mom. "Let's go over to the winery and see what they have to offer."

"Ooh, yes, let's go over to the winery!" said Grandma Helen gleefully clapping her hands.

"What about the boys, shouldn't we wait for them?" I asked.

"Don't worry, I'll call Dad and Ezra and tell them where they can find us," said Mom. "I know they're enjoying themselves and probably won't even realize we're gone."

As we started walking down to the winery, Aunt Christine looked over at Mom with a wicked grin, "You know, maybe we should think about introducing Mom to the world of Instagram and TikTok, it might help her grow her following."

"Do it and die, dear sister," she warned.

CHAPTER FIFTEEN

The next morning began much more pleasantly than the last, as we were finally able to sleep in a bit and enjoy a peaceful and relaxing breakfast in the outer courtyard of our hotel, a 15th-century medieval mill that had recently undergone renovations to resemble a cozy country cottage, complete with rustic stone-paved floors, ivy-covered walls, and an enormous woodburning fireplace. Nestled within the secluded hills of Greve, deep within the Chianti region of Tuscany, the hotel offers the perfect blend of silence, stillness, and tranquility to calm even the loudest of minds, and it is also the exact image I am currently trying to conjure up as I sit here in our rental van listening to my father lose his patience (and temper) over his unsuccessful attempt at navigating the dreaded ZTL zones surrounding Florence's city center.

ZTL, or Zona a Traffico Limitato, for those of you unfamiliar with the term, is a restricted zone that is only allowed to be used by local residents and registered vehicles during certain hours of the day, so if an unauthorized vehicle were to drive through one of these restricted areas at the improper time, the penalty would result in a hefty fine of up to $500.

"Stop telling me to calm down, Olivia!" shouted Dad. "These stupid ZTL zones are all over the damn place and the GPS is telling me to go directly through them." He pulled the van over into a metered parking space as he searched for an alternate route, "How the hell are we supposed to get into the damn parking garage when there are hundreds of ZTL zones completely surrounding it?"

"That's a rhetorical question, right?" mumbled Beau, playing a game on his phone.

"Yes," said Mom. "And please keep the snarky comments to yourself, you know how your father gets whenever he's stressed."

"Party pooper," he muttered.

"This is absolutely asinine!" yelled Dad as he studied the GPS. "There has to be some way to find routes that don't include ZTL's on this stupid thing."

"Honey, you do realize we're sitting in a metered parking space, yes?" asked Mom delicately.

"I don't care if it's metered, it's the only place I could safely pull over," he answered irritably.

"You know, why don't I go ahead and put some money in the meter just to be on the safe side," said Grandpa Anthony.

"No need, we won't be here long enough," said Dad. "I'll figure this thing out in a few minutes."

"But what if the police come over and ticket us?" asked Mom. "Do you really want to get a ticket right now?"

"Not now, Olivia, please," he implored.

"Okay, fine," she shrugged. "It just seems somewhat counterproductive to work so hard to avoid a ZTL fine, yet not worry about a parking fine."

"Seriously, you need to stop," said Dad pointedly. "I'm really trying hard to keep from losing my temper and you are not helping me do that right now."

"God help us when that tsunami decides to hit," mumbled Beau, quietly continuing his game.

"Damnit, this is utterly insane!" said Dad. "Who in their right minds came up with this crap, anyway?"

"We should've just Ubered," muttered Grandma Helen. "It would have been so much easier."

"What is it with you and Uber, anyway?" asked Mom irritably. "Are you earning some sort of commission I'm unaware of?"

"I'm merely making an observation, dear," she replied calmly. "There's no need to get snippy."

"Seriously, how in the hell are we supposed to get into this damn parking garage when we can't even drive on the streets that literally take us there?" asked Dad angrily. "This is completely inane!"

"Um, honey," said Mom quietly. "I think I may actually know what we need to do."

"Not now, Olivia," he huffed. "I'm trying to understand this damn map."

"Okay, fine," she shrugged nonchalantly. "But just so you know, I've figured out how we can avoid getting ticketed."

Dad immediately looked up from his phone, "Okay, you have my attention."

She inhaled a deep breath and said, "Well, apparently, once you pull into the parking garage, a photo of your license plate will be taken, and since the company knows that the only way to their garage is through a ZTL zone, any and all tickets incurred during that time will be null and void." She showed him the screen on her phone, "See, it says so right here."

"Well, why the hell didn't they mention that on the website when I bought the tickets last night?" he barked out. "We could have avoided all of this crap and been there already."

"Oh, thank God," cried out Grandma. "We might actually be able to make our 12:30 reservation for the Academia Gallery after all." She pulled out a small compact and checked her makeup, "You know, The Statue of David, along with all the wine windows, are at the very top of my list, so we really need to make haste, dear."

"Wine windows, really?" asked Aunt Christine. "Not the Duomo, Ponte Vecchio, Piazzale Michelangelo, or any of the other historically significant sights in Florence?"

"Well, yes, those too, I suppose," she said dismissively. "But just think of all of the cute pictures we can get of me ringing the bells outside the wine windows, they will make for a perfect muti-picture Facebook post, don't you think?"

"And just like that, a bimillennium of Roman history is completely overshadowed by a naked marbled man and a wine window with a bell," said Ezra. "What is this world coming to?"

"Okay, so the GPS says we should get to the garage in about 5 minutes," said Dad. "That means we should have just enough time to make our reservation." He carefully pulled out into traffic before glancing back at Mom, "Thank you for finding out about the voided tickets, honey, I'm sorry I got so snippy with you."

"It was a stressful situation, honey," shrugged Mom. "Don't even worry about it."

A few minutes later, we finally located the garage and noticed that there were two lines of cars waiting to enter, one for prepaid tickets and one for non-prepaid tickets.

"What the hell is this?" asked Dad, pulling up behind the last car in the prepaid ticket line.

"It looks like a line," said Ezra.

"I can see it's a line, son, but why is it here?" he asked. "Can we not all just go into the garage and find a parking place, I'm in the prepaid parking line for God's sake."

Just then a small signal light turned green and the next car in line dutifully drove under the raised yellow safety bar and entered into the garage.

"It looks as though you have to wait until someone else leaves before you're even allowed to go in," said Grandpa Anthony. "This may actually take a while."

"Then what's the point of prepaid parking?" asked Dad raising his voice.

Approximately thirty minutes later, we were finally able to enter the garage. Dad obediently followed along the twisting path leading up to the top of the parking garage, but after finding no empty spaces, he immediately made his way back down in search of underground levels that might offer more parking.

"Am I missing something?" he asked. "This thing can't possibly only have three levels."

"I haven't a clue," said Mom. "This whole parking situation is turning out to be a never-ending nightmare."

"Did we maybe miss a turn that takes us down to lower levels or something?" asked Aunt Christine. "I've been looking but haven't been able to find one."

"Maybe there's an attendant we can ask," suggested Ezra. "There's usually some sort of security office in one of these things, right?"

"I honestly don't know," sighed Dad exhaustedly. "Alright, let's just go back up again and see if we can find a vacant spot or someone to help us figure this place out."

Fifteen minutes, and five trips up and down the garage later, Dad angrily peeled out of the parking garage and back onto the street, "I don't believe this!" he yelled. "No parking spaces, no lower levels, no attendants on-site, and a $50 parking pass that is completely obsolete. He threw his phone down onto the console, "And this damn GPS is completely useless."

"You're only now coming to this conclusion?" snarked Beau quietly.

Giving Beau a death glare warning to keep his mouth shut, Mom tried to diffuse the situation, "You know, honey, maybe we should just go back to the hotel, this whole thing is becoming more of a headache than it's worth."

"But what about David and the wine windows?" asked Grandma Helen.

"Mom, I'm sorry, but I think the David ship has sailed," she sighed. "Our reservation is in five minutes and we're at least 20 minutes walking distance away from the city center, there's absolutely no way we can make it." She quickly glanced at Dad in the review mirror, "Honestly, we should probably just cut our losses and go back to the hotel."

"We are not going back to the hotel," said Dad through gritted teeth. "I'll figure something out; you just have to let me do it."

Dad increased his speed and angrily began weaving in and out of traffic.

"Greg, slow down!" said Mom.

"Olivia, I swear to God, if you don't stop, I'm going to pull over and have you drive," he snarled. "I know what I'm doing!"

Grandma Helen leaned in close to Mom and spoke quietly, "You know, dear, considering you never bothered learning how to drive a stick, that really may be in everyone's best interest."

"How are you so calm right now?" asked Mom incredulously. "And for the record, I did try to learn how to drive a stick, I just wasn't any good at it."

"Listen, I've had to deal with plenty of these high-stress situations with your father over the years," she said. "You know, the ones where they can't figure something out so they continue to get angrier with each passing moment until they finally figure it all out and everything is right with the world again?"

"Unfortunately, I'm very familiar, yes," she rolled her eyes.

"Well, the key is to just stay calm and quiet while they yell," she smiled. "They'll eventually come around; they always do."

"Even though it may get us all killed in the process?" asked Mom.

"Oh, don't be so dramatic, Olivia," she scoffed. "Greg is perfectly capable of getting us there in one piece, you just have to let him throw his little tantrum while he does it."

"It's honestly like dealing with a belligerent child," said Mom.

"Actually, darling, I think it's worse because a belligerent child will eventually learn from their mistakes." She looked down at her watch and sighed, "Well, it doesn't look like we're going to be able to make our reservation."

"I'm sorry, Mom, I know you were really looking forward to that," she said.

Grandma Helen leaned in close and whispered conspiratorially, "Honestly, dear, I could care less about seeing The Statue of David."

"What, why?" asked Mom, her brow creased in confusion.

"Oh, I only said I wanted to go there because it was the easiest and least boring of all the options your father gave me," she said. "We only have one day here and I really didn't want to spend it in a bunch of stuffy museums, so I just figured I'd glom onto David since it was quick and easy."

"You know, I realize I should be surprised by this revelation, but sadly, I'm not," said Mom. "You really only care about the wine windows, don't you?"

"And you don't?" she raised her brow knowingly.

"Touché," winked Mom, nodding in agreement.

Just then, Dad abruptly turned into a parking area where a large overweight man was holding a sign advertising available parking. He rolled down his window, paid the fee, and then proceeded to pull into the very first vacant spot he came across.

"Not too shabby, if I do say so myself," he smiled brightly. "Florence, here we come!"

"See, all's well that ends well," grinned Grandma Helen happily. She then glanced over at Dad, "Tell me, dear, do you think we could try and find something a little bit closer; the parking lot is quite long and we have a lot of walking to do today."

"We're staying here, Helen," he said firmly.

"Yes, but…" she continued.

"It practically took an act of God to find this one, we are not leaving," he said, cutting her off abruptly. "Now, I don't know about all of you, but I could use a drink or six."

"Yay, wine windows!" exclaimed Grandma Helen giddily.

CHAPTER SIXTEEN

Ding…ding…ding.

"Is this not absolutely precious?" said Grandma Helen, giddily ringing the small bell outside the first wine window we came across. "It's so tiny and cute!"

Ding…ding…ding.

"Ooh, this is so much fun!" she laughed.

Ding…ding…ding.

"Are you getting any of this, Olivia?" she asked.

"Yes, Mother, I think I have more than enough pictures and video," said Mom. "You can stop ringing the bell now."

"Okay, just one more time!" she exclaimed grabbing the bell rope.

"Let's not and say we did," said Mom, yanking the bell out of her reach. "They probably don't appreciate lunatics continually ringing their bell."

Once we decompressed from the hectic afternoon drive with Dad, we made the brief fifteen-minute walk from the parking area over to Ponte Vecchio, Florence's oldest surviving footbridge that crosses over the Arno River and into the main city center of Florence. The river acts as a divider between the two sides of the city, the Oltrarno District, which literally means "on the other side of Arno," and the Historic Center, which is where most of the museums, historical sites, and Duomo are located.

Ponte Vecchio is one of six bridges that connect the two sides and is the only remaining Florentine bridge to still house many of the shops and apartments originally built upon it. Considered to be one of the most romantic spots in Florence, the bridge offers some of the most spectacular views of the city but is also known to be an incredibly busy area with multiple shopkeepers pandering outrageously expensive jewelry, artwork, and souvenirs to the thousands of daily tourists that walk across it. Add to that an eclectic group of musicians, portraitists, and other entertainers and you can see why Ponte Vecchio has become an incredibly vibrant, eclectic, and bustling tourist spot.

"Ciao tutti!" smiled a young woman opening the wine window. "I see someone is enjoying our little bell."

"Oh, it's absolutely adorable!" exclaimed Grandma Helen.

Ding-

"This is not a toy, Mother," said Mom, grabbing the bell in mid-ding. "Have some self-control, please."

Grandma Helen promptly stuck her tongue out at Mom and then mischievously winked over at the attendant who was watching in amusement, "Don't mind her, she's still sober."

"Well, we need to fix that, then, don't we," she winked back.

After we ordered our wine, we found two small tables on the opposite side of the street and took a seat. Mom, Aunt Christine, Grandma Helen, and I opted to share a bottle of Prosecco, while Dad, Grandpa Anthony, and Ezra ordered a bottle of a local Chianti. Beau actually lucked out this time and was able to enjoy an ice-cold bottle of Coca-Cola, which he promptly downed before immediately ordering another.

"So, exactly how many wine windows are there in Florence," I asked. "Does anyone know?"

"There are actually 285 wine windows," said Dad. "And half of them reside right here in Old Town."

"How did you even know that," asked Mom, her interest piqued.

"I did my research," he smiled. "I also know that wine windows became popular around the 16th century when local winemakers would sell their wine directly out of their homes rather than out of shops so that they wouldn't have to pay taxes." He took a sip of wine and then continued, "And they were also really useful during the bubonic plague outbreak that spread throughout northern Italy because it limited contact between buyers and sellers. With the window acting as a barrier, there was a lower chance of contagion, and with that, fewer deaths."

"Yeah, but what about the money, wouldn't that be contaminated too?" asked Beau.

"That's actually a good question, Beau," he said. "Apparently, whenever money was collected, it would be placed on a metal pallet, doused

in vinegar, which of course acts as a disinfectant, and then dried. It's all pretty ingenious if you ask me."

"Wow, that's really interesting," said Mom. "I had absolutely no idea that's how it all started."

"That is so cool!" exclaimed Beau. "Imagine still being able to get drunk when people are dropping like flies and dying all around you; I mean, that had to have been good for morale, you know?"

"Well, I don't care about all that history, but I do find them absolutely adorable," said Grandma Helen. "Plus they have a cheerful little bell you can ring, who wouldn't love something like that?"

"I would imagine someone who doesn't enjoy hearing it rung 50 times within a sixty second period," answered Aunt Christine.

As we sat along the cobbled stone streets sipping our wine, Grandma Helen sighed contentedly as she poured herself another glass of Prosecco.

"It's just lovely here isn't it?" she said. "You know, I hear there are some amazing rooftop bars all around the city of Florence, maybe we should swing by one for a drink so we can get a bird's eye view of the city."

"Ooh, I would love to see the city from above," said Mom. "I bet it's simply stunning."

"Can we at least eat something first?" asked Beau. "I'm starving and breakfast has long worn off thanks to Dad's catastrophic two-hour parking debacle."

"I eventually found parking," he combated. "And for the record, it wasn't two hours, it was just under, thank you very much."

"Hey, isn't that famous sandwich shop here, Addie?" asked Ezra. "The one you saw on TikTok?"

"All'Antico Vinaio, yes," I nodded. "There are actually quite a few locations throughout the city, and I don't think any of them are very far from where we are so we should be able to get to one relatively quickly."

"Sandwiches?" snarled Grandma Helen. "We're in Florence, you don't eat sandwiches in Florence."

"Well, whatever we decide to do, let's not eat too much," said Aunt Christine. "Jack made reservations for us at his friend's restaurant at 6:30, remember?"

"Ugh, he's such a cretin," sighed Grandma Helen. "Do we really have to go?"

"Yes, Mother, we do," she answered.

"You know, I've heard some wonderful things about that sandwich shop too, Addie," said Grandpa Anthony. "In fact, Donny and his wife ate there when they were here visiting and both said it was fantastic, although he did mention having to stand in line for a while."

"Stand in line for a sandwich?" asked Grandma Helen. "Are you serious?"

"I hear they're actually really good, Grandma," I said. "Everyone on TikTok is raving about them."

"What exactly is this TikTok you and your brothers keep talking about?" she asked.

"Nothing," interjected Mom, practically choking on her wine. "It's just something the kids like to watch from time to time."

Mom had absolutely no intention of introducing Grandma Helen to the world of TikTok, and from the death glare she was currently giving me, Beau, and Ezra, it would appear that we were to keep that introduction from happening as well.

"I tell you what, why don't we all finish our drinks and then go grab a sandwich," said Dad, pulling out his phone. "I'll see if I can locate the nearest one to us and pull up a map to help get us there."

"Ugh, fine," relented Grandma Helen. "I may as well get another glass of Prosecco to wash it all down with; does anyone else want anything?"

"No, thank you," we answered.

"And please don't ring that bell again," said Mom. "The window's open, they'll see you coming."

"Yes, dear," she nodded convivially. "I'll be sure to be on my best behavior."

"You know that means she won't be, right?" said Ezra.

We watched her walk over to the window, place her order, and wave back at us before deciding to deliberately taunt Mom with the act of pretending to touch the bell rope. While she waited for the attendant to pour her wine, she slowly inched her finger closer and closer to the bell, much like that of a mischievous child, and stared defiantly over at Mom.

"Ring that bell again, Mother, and I'll ring you," called out Mom.

With a devilish grin, Grandma Helen purposefully reached under the bell, grabbed hold of the dangling chord, and tugged.

Ding...ding...ding.

***

Once Dad was able to locate the nearest sandwich shop, we made the ten-minute walk over to where it was and found that the line wasn't too bad, so we waited another 10 minutes and then eventually placed our order. Once we finished our sandwiches, we decided to walk around the city and take in the sights, swinging by a few more wine windows as we did, before making our way over to the infamous Duomo, which is one of the main landmarks of the city.

The Cathedral of Santa Maria Del Fiore, known also as the Duomo, is quite honestly one of the most breathtaking sights I have ever seen. Standing tall above Florence's city center, with its magnificent Renaissance, red-tiled dome, the Duomo is considered to be the third largest cathedral in the world, its stunning Florentine Gothic and Italian Renaissance-styled architecture drawing millions of visitors to Florence each year. Covered in a decorative mix of pink, white, and green marble, this massive structure was initially built during the end of the 13th century by an Italian architect named Arnolfo di Cambio, with the famous red dome, designed by Filippo Brunelleschi, being added to the structure almost two centuries later. This towering architectural wonder was simply stunning, and I found myself mesmerized by its beauty.

"Ugh, thank God we don't have to go up into that thing," said Grandma Helen, breaking my train of thought. "463 steps, can you even imagine having to climb all that?"

"I bet it's worth it," I said. "The views must be amazing."

"Yes, well, we can get some of those very same views high up on a rooftop bar, which by the way, is sounding quite appealing to me right about now," she said.

Mom sidled up to the two of us and looked up in awe, "Isn't it breathtaking?"

"Eh," shrugged Grandma Helen.

"You can't possibly already be bored with this, Mother," she said. "This is beyond beautiful, even you have to admit that."

"We've been standing here for over thirty minutes," she said. "Yes, it's beautiful, but now what?"

"Mom, do you have any idea how much history is standing before you right now?" asked Mom incredulously. "How much history is everywhere around you, for that matter?"

"I'm aware," she said. "I just don't need hours upon hours to experience it, that's all. It's like when your father insisted on taking us to see the Grand Canyon when you and your sister were little. He made us stand there for an entire hour staring at a bunch of eroded red rocks when in reality, we could have left after five minutes, had a nice lunch, and been on our merry way."

"You know, you never cease to amaze me," said Mom shaking her head.

"Thank you, dear,' she smiled. "I am rather unpredictable."

"That wasn't a compliment," she retorted.

"Hey, do you think anyone would mind if Anthony and I made a quick detour over to the pipe shop?" interrupted Dad. "One of the guys in my pipe group suggested it and it's literally only a two-minute walk from here."

"Yeah, that's fine," said Mom. "Once everyone reconvenes, we'll just head over that way." She pulled out her phone and handed it to him, "Would you mind just bringing it up on my map so that I know where we're going?"

He quickly entered the information, pulled up the map, and kissed her, "Thanks, honey!"

"Ugh, now we have to add pipes to all of this?" whined Grandma Helen. "When are we going to do something fun, I'm tired of sightseeing."

"Hey, everyone's been humoring you with your wine windows," said Mom. "Now it's time for you to return the favor."

"Yes, but when I'm drinking wine I'm happy and occupied," she said. "What exactly am I supposed to do in a pipe shop, it's so dull and full of tobacco."

"You know, someday you're going to have to grow up and realize that the entire world does not revolve solely around you, Mother," countered Mom. "There are seven other people on this vacation, each with varying interests, so you're just going to have to suck it up and play nice, okay?"

"Okay, fine, I'll go to the pipe shop," she capitulated. "There's no need to get upset."

"Hey, Ollie, I think I may have found you the perfect magnet for Florence," said Aunt Christine walking towards us. "It's a painted representation of the Duomo overlooking all the rooftops in the city, I really think you're going to like it."

"Ooh, show me!" said Mom, clapping her hands excitedly.

My Mother is currently on the hunt to find the perfect refrigerator magnet from each Italian city we visit, with the eventual goal of covering her entire refrigerator in magnets from every place she and Dad will one day visit once Beau graduates. This trip to Italy is her starting point, and she has been collecting them like a mad woman.

"Oh dear God, who in their right mind gets excited about a refrigerator magnet?" asked Grandma Helen. "Your mother is nothing if not pedestrian."

"Um, if I'm not mistaken, the ringing of a bell excited you earlier, Grandma, so the same could be said about you," I pointed out.

"Darling, that bell led to wine, and as we all know, wine is divine," she smiled good-naturedly. "Speaking of which, I think it's time for another glass, don't you?"

"No, I think I'm good for right now," I said.

Once Mom bought her magnet, we quickly rounded up Beau and Ezra and made our way over to the pipe shop. Seeing that Dad and Grandpa Anthony were deeply engrossed in the hundreds of shelves of pipes on display, we left the boys with them and then headed across the alley to a quaint little wine shop where we could sit and wait for them to finish.

About an hour later, they finally exited the shop with two small bags and cheerfully made their way over to us.

"That was an amazing experience," said Dad. "Thank you so much for being patient, we really appreciate it." He set his bag on the table and pulled out his phone, "It says that restaurant is only a few blocks from here, so if we leave now, we should be able to make our reservation in plenty of time."

"Did you find everything you were looking for, dear?" asked Grandma Helen.

"That, and then some," he smiled. "I think Anthony and I were both like kids in a candy store."

"He more so than me," winked Grandpa Anthony. "I practically had to drag him out of there kicking and screaming."

"Actually, it was more like Beau and me having to drag the two of you out, Grandpa," said Ezra. "Speak the truth."

"Well, maybe I overexaggerated that last part just a bit," he smiled sheepishly.

After making the brief walk over to the restaurant, Trattoria Toscana, we were immediately greeted by a young woman standing behind a tall wooden lectern. She asked us what name the reservation was under and then quickly excused herself to make sure that our table was ready.

"Wow, this is really nice," said Mom admiring the vestibule.

"Jack says that they serve the best Florentine steak in the city," said Aunt Christine. "He also said that it's incredibly hard to get reservations, which is why he made one for us."

"Jack says this, Jack says that," mimicked Grandma Helen irritably under her breath. "Jack's an ass."

The young woman eventually came back and then led us through the main part of the restaurant and up a flight of stairs to a private dining area that was set off toward the back of the restaurant. Upon entering, we saw a long rectangular dining table set beautifully with eight place settings, three decorative vases filled with sunflowers, and two bottles of Prosecco chilling in tall silver ice buckets at each end of the table. In the center sat an oval platter piled high with select meats and cheeses flanked with two baskets of freshly baked focaccia bread. As the young woman ushered us to our seats, she informed us that Antonio, the restaurant's owner would be with us shortly, and to please feel free to help ourselves.

"Sweet!" exclaimed Beau.

"This is incredible," said Ezra.

"You know, Jack may not be such a bad guy after all," said Beau, happily piling his plate with meat. "I mean, yeah, the guy's not trustworthy, but I definitely respect his connections."

"Did Jack really set all of this up?" asked Mom.

"I honestly have no idea," said Aunt Christine bewildered. "I just thought he was making a reservation for us."

Just then a distinguished looking gentleman in an expensively tailored navy-blue suit walked in. He was incredibly handsome and looked to be somewhere in his late forties with dark hair and a smile that practically lit up the room.

"Good evening," he said. "My name is Antonio Rossi, and I am the owner and manager of Trattoria Toscana. I wanted to personally come in and welcome all of you and also let you know that we have created a special preplanned menu in honor of your visit that will include many of our most popular and enticing dishes as well as our famous Florentine steak, which I am proud to say is quite honestly the best you will find here in Firenze." He gestured toward the platter on the table, "Please help yourself to as much taglieri e formaggi as you would like and be sure to have a glass or two of wine, the Brunello is one of my favorites."

"Thank you so much, Antonio," said Aunt Christine. "Jack has spoken very highly of you; we truly appreciate you putting all of this together for us."

"The honor is all mine," he smiled. "Jack has become a good friend over the years, so I was more than happy to accommodate his request to make this a memorable evening for all of you." He lifted up one of the menus sitting on the table, "Also, if you happen to see something else you'd like to try, please just let me know and I'll be sure we bring that out as well."

"We really appreciate that, Antonio, thank you," smiled Dad.

"My pleasure," he nodded. "Oh, and before I forget, this entire evening is courtesy of Jack, so there will be no need to pay for anything at the end of the night."

After registering our surprise at this recent revelation, Grandma Helen, who had been silently reading the wine menu, looked up at Antonio and smiled effervescently as she pointed to one of the listed wines, "You know, dear, I remember Jack raving about this 2006 Massetto Toscana a while back, why don't you go ahead and bring us two bottles of that and we'll see if there's anything else that strikes our fancy."

"I'd be happy to," he bowed slightly.

"I don't remember Jack ever mentioning a wine like that," said Aunt Christine. "He wasn't the most savvy wine drinker to begin with."

Mom glanced down at the menu Grandma Helen was holding, "Mom, that's over $1500 a bottle," she hissed. "You can't order that; the bill will be exorbitant!"

"That man hurt my baby, Olivia, the hell I can't," she growled.

CHAPTER SEVENTEEN

"Churchill, please don't look at Mommy that way," pleaded Mom. "We're halfway through our vacation, I'll be back before you know it, I promise."

Churchill's droopy jowls and disinterested face filled the screen as Mom unnecessarily reassured him of her imminent return. She once again usurped Aunt Christine's phone call with Brian and was currently trying to get his attention as he carelessly licked his front left paw.

"Brian, do you think you could get the screen a little bit closer to him?" she asked. "I don't think he can see me."

"He can see you, Olivia, believe me," he answered patiently. "I think he's just tired and ready to go to sleep, that's all."

"Or he's finally come to the realization that you've completely lost your mind and wants absolutely nothing to do with your kind of crazy," said Ezra. "At least, that's what I'd be thinking."

"I didn't ask for your opinion, Ezra," she said irritably.

"Yes, but I have such insight and awareness, it would be a shame to not share it with those less fortunate," he snarked. "It's my gift and my curse."

"Okay, may I please have my phone back?" interrupted Aunt Christine, holding her hand out expectantly. "I'd really like to talk with my fiancée now."

We were currently on the train headed for Rome, and before Aunt Christine could even issue a proper greeting to Brian, the phone was immediately swiped out of her hand so that Mom could receive her daily dose of disregard from the only being on Earth able to get away with it. Don't get me wrong, Churchill loves her in his own way, but his heart is fickle and predominantly food-guided, so it would seem that Brian, his current caregiver, is the only one worthy of receiving any and all of his fleeting attention.

"Okay, fine," said Mom, reluctantly handing the phone back to her.

"Thank you," said Aunt Christine, placing an earbud back into her ear.

"Just be sure to give him lots of hugs and kisses for me and make sure he has his blankie nearby," she yelled out. "Oh, and also make sure he's getting his daily chewy, he loves those!"

"He's got his blankie and has already had his daily chewy," said Aunt Christine. "May I please talk with Brian now?"

"Yes, of course, I'm sorry," said Mom penitently.

We had been on the train for close to an hour and were excited to get into Rome so that we could spend the majority of the day sightseeing. We had spent our last day in Tuscany with a visit to Montepulciano, a small medieval hilltop town located deep within the heart of Val d'Orcia. It is a stunning area surrounded by large vineyards, olive groves, and waves of rolling hills that seem to go on forever. We walked around the town and visited numerous small shops and boutiques. We even found a local wine shop that was built directly over a working archaeological dig, complete with plexiglass floors that allowed visitors to see the excavated site. This, of course, had Mom completely geeked out because it combined two of her favorite things, wine and archaeology, But it also made it practically impossible to get her to willingly do anything else. She eventually capitulated, though, and we were finally able to finish the day at a local restaurant that served some of the most amazing spaghetti alla puttanesca I'd ever had, but don't ever expect me to admit that in front of my grandfather, he would never forgive me.

"Okay, so once the train arrives, there should be a shuttle waiting to take us to the hotel," said Grandpa Anthony. "I suggest we drop off our bags and then head back out, we're only in Rome for two days, so we'll want to see as much as we possibly can."

"Where are we staying again, dear?" asked Grandma Helen. "The Alpha, the Omega, I can't seem to remember."

"The Aleph Hotel," he said. "It's in a fairly central location, so it should make getting to tomorrow's tours relatively easy."

Grandpa Anthony had booked two different tours for tomorrow, one for the Colosseum, Roman Forum, and Palatine Hill during the morning, and then one later in the afternoon for the Capuchin Crypts and underground Catacombs, both of which I was really looking forward to.

As we exited the Roma Termini train station, we immediately located the shuttle that would take us over to the hotel. After a short 5-minute drive, we exited the shuttle and immediately made our way into the lobby of the hotel where two bellmen greeted us before offering to retrieve our luggage. We then followed Mom and Dad over to the concierge desk and waited patiently behind them while they checked us in.

As a favor to Grandpa Anthony, and because Dad is a Hilton Honor member, he graciously offered to use his hotel points to pay for the rooms, which not only helped lift the financial burden off of him and Grandma Helen but also enabled us to stay in a very swanky and ritzy hotel.

"Good afternoon, and welcome to the Aleph," smiled a young man behind the counter. "My name is Matteo; how may I help you?"

"Good afternoon," replied Dad. "We have a reservation under Jenkins for four separate rooms."

Matteo quickly tapped a few keys on his computer and then looked back up at Mom and Dad.

"Mr. and Mrs. Jenkins, yes, we are so honored to have you join us here at the Aleph Roma," he beamed. "If you'll excuse me just a moment, my manager has requested to speak with you." He pointed to the door behind him, "I'll just go and get him."

"Greg, what did you do," asked Mom ominously. "Why does he want to talk to us?"

"I didn't do anything," he shrugged defensively. "I checked in exactly like I would at any other hotel."

"Oh my God, what if they can't accommodate us?" whispered Mom. "What if there aren't enough rooms?"

"Would you stop, you're being ridiculous," he said.

"What if I have we end up having to share a room with my mother?" she hissed. "Greg, I don't think I can do that; we're going to have to go someplace else."

"You do realize I can hear you, dear, yes?" asked Grandma Helen. "And for the record, I'd like to state that you're no picnic either."

"Calm down, Olivia, I made these reservations months ago and even have the confirmation number on my phone, see?" he said. "You have absolutely nothing to worry about."

"Mr. and Mrs. Jenkins, hello!" said a tall lanky man in a three-piece suit. He smiled warmly and began introducing himself, "My name is Lorenzo Lombardi and I am the manager here at the Aleph Roma; I wanted to personally let you know that we are honored to be hosting you and your family over the next few days."

"It's so nice to meet you," said Dad, shaking his hand.

"I hope you don't mind, but I asked Matteo to notify me of your arrival so that I could greet you and personally escort you to your rooms," he smiled. "I also wanted to let you know that we have upgraded your room to the Basilio, Prestige suite, which actually has two large bedrooms, so if you'd like, we'll be more than happy to cancel one of the reservations so that you can share the suite with an extra set of guests."

"Oh wow, yes, that would be wonderful, thank you," said Dad.

"I'll see to it immediately," he bowed his head slightly. "Now, if you'll allow me a few minutes, I'll go and get the keys so that we can get you settled in quickly."

As soon as Lorenzo turned to leave, Mom leaned in close to Dad, "Please tell me you're not thinking of offering that extra room to my parents."

"They're the ones paying for this entire trip, Olivia, it would be rude not to," he said. "Besides, it's only for two nights, it won't be that bad."

"You know my Mother, Greg, she's the queen of high maintenance, of course it's going to be-"

"Upgrade?" interrupted Grandma Helen. "Did I hear that correctly, dear?"

"Yes, Mother, you did," said Mom.

"And who are the fortunate souls that were upgraded, exactly?" she asked.

"Uh, that would be me and Greg," she said.

"And why, pray tell, would they choose to upgrade the two of you and not the rest of us?" she asked.

"Honey, you can't expect them to upgrade all eight of us to a suite," said Grandpa Anthony. "That wouldn't make much sense."

I understand that, Anthony," she replied. "I'm just curious as to why it was specifically Greg and Olivia that were upgraded and not anyone else."

"It's probably because I'm a lifetime Diamond member and have a lot of status with Hilton Hotels," said Dad. "Also, I know that when hotels aren't completely booked, they tend to upgrade their Diamond members as an added perk, so with the rooms being under my points and my name, I'm the one who gets the upgrade."

Before Grandma Helen had a chance to respond, we could see Lorenzo making his way back over to us.

"Okay, I have the keys, so if you follow me, I'll be happy to escort you up to your rooms," he smiled.

As they walked behind him, Dad whispered into Mom's ear, "Listen, you and I both know this is the right thing to do, so you may as well get on board because I'm letting them have the room."

"Okay, fine," she relented. "The woman was bound to weasel her way into it anyway."

We followed Lorenzo to the elevators and watched him press the call button, "We'll be sending your luggage up shortly, so just call down to the concierge whenever you're ready and let us know which room belongs to whom."

We rode the elevator to the top floor, exited, and then continued to follow Lorenzo as he led us down a long hallway that ended in a tall set of white double doors. He gently slipped the key into the scanner, opened the door, and then stepped aside to allow us entry.

"This is our finest suite," he said. "As you can see, it is quite spacious and has a lovely view of the city." He then gestured toward one of the bedrooms, "Come, let me show you around."

To say the suite was beautiful would be an understatement. It was beyond impressive, with an enormous living and dining area separating two large bedrooms, each sumptuously furnished with a king-sized bed, a sizeable lounging area, and a giant walk-in closet. There were also two private bathrooms with his and her sinks, heated tile floors, and two full-sized showers, both equipped with cascading waterfall showerheads that practically rained water from the ceiling. In addition, there was also a tall shelving unit immediately to the left of the vanity that held two folded plush white robes, two sets of terrycloth slippers, and a variety of expensive soaps, lotions, and shampoos.

After making our way back into the living area, Lorenzo pointed over to a large black espresso machine, wine refrigerator, and fully stocked bar sitting to the right of an enormous fireplace, "Please feel free to help yourself to as much coffee, wine, and spirits as you'd like, it'll be restocked daily throughout your entire stay here."

"Oh my God this is absolutely amazing!" said Mom. "I'm not ever going to want to leave the room!"

"Wow, this place is huge!" exclaimed Beau. "Dang, Dad, you and I might need to start taking a few more father-and-son trips, this is insane."

"This rarely, if ever, happens, Beau, so don't get too excited," he chuckled.

Lorenzo gestured toward a large square coffee table in the center of the room, "And as you can see, we have also set out a complementary tray of various chocolates, sweets, and of course, a chilled bottle of champagne, to celebrate your arrival and stay with us here at the Aleph." He set down three sets of key cards on the table and then continued, "Here are your keys, and as always, if you need anything, please feel free to reach out and let us know. Breakfast will be served downstairs between 7:00 and 10:00, and we also have a full bar downstairs behind the concierge desk as well as a rooftop bar, restaurant, and pool area that offer a phenomenal view of the Piazza del Colosseo, which is where the Colosseum is located."

"Thank you so much, Lorenzo," said Dad, shaking his hand. "I can't tell you how much we appreciate all of this."

"Yes, of course," he smiled. "Again, we hope you enjoy your stay with us."

"Well, I'm thinking we're off to a pretty banging start with all this, Lorenzo," said Beau, popping a piece of chocolate into his mouth.

As soon as Lorenzo had closed the door behind him, Grandma Helen immediately began clapping her hands in excitement, "Oh, this is going to be so much fun!" she exclaimed. "Anthony, would you please call down to the concierge and tell them where to send our luggage, I need to fix my hair and refresh my makeup."

"Yes, of course, dear," he smiled.

"Okay, well, I think I'll go ahead and freshen up a little myself before we head back out," said Aunt Christine. She handed me a key card, "Here Addie, if I'm not mistaken, I think we're the first room on the left."

"Okay, thanks," I said. "I'll be there in just a minute."

"Olivia, did you see the bathrobes, slippers, and heated towel racks in the bathroom?" asked Grandma Helen. "Oh, this suite is beyond what I expected it to be, it's simply spectacular!"

I did, yes," nodded Mom. "Although, I am curious as to why you automatically think it's you that will be staying in the suite and not one the others."

"Don't be daft, darling," she laughed. "You and I both know that your father and I are the only logical choice."

"Not to mention Greg already told us it was ours when you were checking out the other bedroom," winked Grandpa Anthony.

"Oh, he did, did he?" said Mom, raising a brow in amusement.

"Yes, he did," answered Grandma Helen, raising one of her own. "He's a wonderful son-in-law and apparently cares more about my comfort than my own daughter does."

"It's not like you were preparing to sleep in a hostel, Mother," she rolled her eyes. "Your comfort was never in question and you know it."

"Well, it certainly isn't now, is it?" she smiled. "Excuse me, dear, I need to go and make my room selection, ta-ta!"

Mom sat down on the couch next to Beau, who was happily munching on a pastry, and watched as Dad poured bourbon into a tumbler, "Well, I see your father has already made himself at home."

"Do you blame him?" asked Beau. "The man just made a deal with the devil; he deserves a drink."

"What in the world are you talking about?" asked Mom. "What deal with the devil?"

"You know, his ill-fated sleepover with Grandma," he shrugged. Two uninterrupted nights having to deal with her would make even a prohibitionist want to drink; he's probably just gearing himself up for the inevitable."

"Well, you do seem to make a good point, I'll give you that," she said.

"Of course I do," he smiled, picking his key card up from the table. "Don't worry, Mom, you'll survive this, I have faith."

"Need a drink?" asked Dad, holding out a glass.

"Actually, I think I need a distillery," she sighed.

Chapter Eighteen

"Okay let me see that one," said Grandma Helen, sideling up next to Mom. She looked down at the image on the screen and shook her head slowly, "No, I don't think that one's going to work either."

"I'm not taking any more pictures, Mother, the ten I've already taken will work just fine," said Mom. "Besides, we probably need to start heading back to the kiosk so we don't miss the beginning of the tour."

Grandma Helen had surprisingly persuaded Mom to step away from the tour's meeting point in order to take a few pictures in front of the Colosseum, and since I had somehow unwittingly become the photographer's assistant, I ended up being dragged along too.

"Darling, we have fifteen minutes before the tour even starts, we'll be fine," she said dismissively. "Now, let's just move five steps over this way because the lighting is better and it won't make me look so washed out."

"Grandma, you look beautiful in these pictures," I said. "You really don't need to take anymore."

"Thank you, darling, I appreciate you saying that, but I still think it would be wise to take a few more just to be on the safe side." The words had barely left her mouth when her face lit up with an entirely new thought, "You know what, Olivia, I have an even better idea, why don't you get a picture of me with my beautiful granddaughter, that way my followers will be able to see me out and about exploring with my family."

"Okay, fine," sighed Mom. "But after this, I'm done."

As Mom started taking pictures of me and Grandma Helen, an older looking gentleman walked up behind her to offer his assistance, "You know, I'd be happy to take a picture of all three of you, if you'd like."

"Oh, it's okay," smiled Mom. "We're just about done here anyway."

"Actually, that would be wonderful, dear,!" exclaimed Grandma Helen. "Olivia, I'm sure everyone would love to see you in some of my photo's too; you know, the face behind the lens and all." She then leaned in close to me, "Plus everyone needs to see how important family is to me, the theater puts on a ton of family-friendly productions, so a picture with you and your mother will be a perfect way to demonstrate that."

"Okay, well, I guess we'll take you up on the offer, then," said Mom. She slowly handed the phone to him, "It's already set up so that the entire Colosseum can be seen in the background, so all you really need to do is just center us in the picture and then press this round button right here at the bottom of the screen."

"Sounds simple enough." He waited for Mom to pose alongside me and Grandma Helen and then said, "Okay, everyone, smile for the camera!"

As we stood there smiling, he lowered the phone and began curiously inspecting it, "I'm so sorry, but I think I just pressed something I wasn't supposed to."

Mom walked back over to him and kindly retrieved the phone from his hand.

"I think you may have exited out of the camera by accident," she said. "But I've brought it back up so you should be good now."

"Oh, okay, thank you," he smiled graciously. "Alright everyone, let's try this again, say cheese!"

"Cheese!" we said in unison.

"Oh dear, now it doesn't seem to be taking the picture," he said, his brow creasing in concern. "I'm pushing the button, but the screen just keeps flip-flopping back and forth between the two of us."

"Here, let me show you how to do it again," said Mom. "These phones can be tricky."

"No, I think I'll be able to figure it out," he waved her off. "I'm just going to need a minute."

"Oh, for God's sake, we could have been sculpted by now," snarked Grandma Helen.

"Shh, keep your voice down, Mother, he's only trying to help," chided Mom.

"It's a camera phone, Olivia, not rocket science," she said irritably. "Even an untrained monkey could figure it out."

"Would you please stop?" said Mom. "If he can't figure it out within the next few seconds, we'll just tell him not to worry about it, but until then, play nice."

"Oh, wait, I think I've got it now!" he exclaimed excitedly. "I was pressing the wrong button, but I think I know what to do now." He lifted the phone up again, "Okay, everyone, smile big for the camera!"

After he had finally taken our picture, we quickly thanked him and then rushed back over to the kiosk where the rest of the family, and a few recent newcomers, stood waiting. The group had ended up being relatively small, mainly consisting of our family, a young couple on their honeymoon, and another middle-aged couple, whose husband proudly wore a shirt that read, "I left my heart at Hooters, just don't tell my wife."

"Hooters, really?" said Grandma Helen irritably. "Ugh, why do people insist on wearing things that are so indecorous and insipid, it's like their advertising their stupidity."

"Just keep your opinions to yourself, please," said Mom. "Not everyone likes to dress to the nines like you do."

"Yes, well, they should, the world would be a much prettier place if they did," she said. "You know, it never ceases to amaze me how many people there are in this world with little to no taste, it's honestly quite disheartening."

"Oh, my gosh, I love that shirt!" exclaimed Beau. "Mom, I'm totally going to have to get one of those when I get back home."

"I rest my case," she sighed. "Okay, where is this person, I'm tired of standing around."

"Be patient, Mother, they'll be here when they get here," said Mom.

Just then a woman in her mid-fifties, who was holding a tall white pole with a red flag attached, approached our group confidently.

"Good morning, everyone!" she smiled. "My name is Elena Barbieri and I am one of the tour guides with Tour Roma. I am so happy to have all of you join me today and I cannot wait to get started, but before we do, please allow me to give you just a little bit of background information about myself." She lowered her red flag and continued, "I was born here in Roma and have lived here all my life; in fact, I grew up just a few blocks away from where we're standing right now. Over the years, I have made it my mission to become well-versed in all areas of Ancient Roman culture and lifestyle so that I can share it with those of you who come to visit. I have been doing these types of tours for just over ten years now, but prior to this, I was a schoolteacher, and the subject I loved teaching most was history. As a result, I can assure you that you will be learning quite a lot over these next few hours and will be leaving here with your head full of knowledge. I do ask that you please pay attention and keep your talking at a minimum so that others will not be disturbed as we take this remarkable walk through Ancient Roman history together."

She paused momentarily as a young woman began handing out one-sided headphones.

"Now, as you all know, we will be touring the Colosseum, Palatine Hill, and Roman Forum, today, so wearing the headphones that Francesca is currently handing out to all of you will enable you to hear me as we tour around all the amazing ancient ruins within the three sites. Please be sure to pay careful attention and stay close to the group because it's quite easy to get lost in these crowds." She lifted the flagpole in her hand, "And as you can see, I have this tall red flag, so if you do happen to find yourself lost, just look for the red flag and you'll know exactly where to find us."

She clipped a small microphone to the collar of her shirt, "Now, before we get started, please place the headphone on the outer portion of your ear and then let me know if you can hear me."

"Ugh, do I really have to wear this thing?" asked Grandma Helen. "It's clashing with my earring and not fitting correctly."

"Just take the earring off, then," said Mom.

"Have you completely lost your mind?" she hissed. "You know I never leave the house without earrings, and I absolutely refuse to take one off, that will only make me look lopsided and out of proportion."

"Then take them both off," shrugged Mom. "I highly doubt anyone will even notice anyway."

"Yes, but I'll notice," she said adamantly. "And then my entire morning will be ruined."

"Well, I'm not sure what you want me to do about it, Mother, you either wear the headphone or you don't," said Mom.

"You know what, I'm sure I'll be able to hear her just fine without it," she said. "Besides it's not like I'm all that interested in any of this anyway."

"Yeah, God forbid you actually learn something while you're here," snarked Mom.

"You know, the crowd's probably going to be drowning out her voice, Grandma, so you may really want to think about wearing it," I said.

"But I don't want-"

"Excuse me, are you having a problem with your headphone?" interrupted Elena. "Is it not working?"

"No, no, it's fine," smiled Mom. "We've got it all under control, thank you."

Mom turned around and immediately stared daggers down at Grandma Helen, "Alright listen, I refuse to allow you to make a spectacle of yourself, Mother, so just put the damn headphone on and stop being difficult. I've been looking forward to this tour for months and I refuse to miss any of it because of your inability to go along to get along, do you understand?"

"Okay, fine, you don't have to get so snippy about it," she said defensively. "I had no idea it was so important to you."

As Mom turned to make her way over to Aunt Christine, Beau amiably sidled up next to her, "Try not to take it personally, Grandma, she acts exactly the same way when she makes me watch documentaries for school, she's kind of a dweeb, if you know what I mean."

"Kind of?" she raised her brow questioningly.

"Okay, maybe more of an obsessive geek on steroids, but you didn't hear any of that from me." He adjusted his headphones, "My mouth gets me into enough trouble as it is, I don't need any extra help."

"Not to worry, dear, your secret's safe with me," she smiled, patting him on the shoulder.

Once we were through security, Elena quickly launched into her lecture, giving a detailed history of the Colosseum including, when and how it was built, the ways in which it was used, and how at the height of the Roman Empire, it ultimately served as the number one form of entertainment in helping to amuse a bloodthirsty and violent Roman populace.

Over the years, I have learned a lot about the history of Ancient Rome, but I was actually surprised at how much more I learned by simply taking this tour with Elena. For example, I was interested to learn that the Colosseum was active for four centuries before the struggles of the Western Roman Empire (and the gradual change in the public's taste for bloodlust) finally put an end to all gladiatorial combat. I was also interested to learn that upon its abandonment, crucial pieces from the Colosseum were quarried in order to aid in numerous building projects for the Catholic church, including the Cathedral of St. Peter, the Palazzo Venezia, and many of the defense fortifications that were built along the Tiber River. In fact, by the time the 20th century rolled around, nearly two-thirds of the original structure, including the arena's 50,000 marble seats and countless decorative details were destroyed due to weather erosion, natural disaster, neglect, and of course, rampant vandalism.

Once we finished touring the Colosseum, we made a brief stop at the Arch of Constantine, one of the largest and best-preserved arches in Rome, before heading over to Palatine Hill, the birthplace of the country's capital. Dad had been taking pictures of the arch when he realized that both Beau and Grandma Helen were missing, so he quickly walked over to where Ezra and I were standing to see if we knew anything.

"Hey, have either of you seen Beau or your Grandmother anywhere?" asked Dad. "I can't seem to find them anywhere."

"I think they veered off to get some kind of Italian ice or something," said Ezra. "They should be back any minute."

"They did?" asked Dad in surprise. "Together?"

"Yeah, I think they both needed a break, especially after being called out by Elena for talking too much and not listening," he said.

Elena's schoolteacher roots had been on full display throughout the entire tour of the Colosseum as she reprimanded, shooed away, or admonished, anyone found sitting on the ruins (not from our group, of course), loitering in her lecture space, or talking, even for the briefest of moments, during her lengthy disquisitions.

"Well, they'd better hurry up, then," said Dad. "I don't want to make Elena upset; she might just slap the back of our hands with a ruler if we disobey her rules any more than we already have."

As we stood there waiting, we eventually heard Beau and Grandma Helen walk up behind us laughing uncontrollably as they both tried mimicking Elena with terrible Italian accents.

"Little boy," said Beau. "Please focus and pay attention!"

"Signora, please put the headphone on so that you can hear my words,'" parodied Grandma Helen, tapping at her right ear. "You must listen so that you can understand."

"No, no, no, I said to go this way," said Beau. "Why do you not follow my red flag, do you not see it?"

"There will be no picture taking times right now," said Grandma Helen, waggling her finger. "I have better places for you to take them, so please wait until I stop and show you."

"Having fun?" asked Dad.

"Oh hello, dear, yes, we are," smiled Grandma Helen. "Beau and I decided we needed to take a break from little miss fascist, so we decided to treat ourselves to some Italian ice."

"Okay, well, fun times over, we really need to catch up with the group," he said. "I don't want to know what she'll do if she finds us missing."

"Chicken," teased Beau. "It's not like she can do anything to us, we paid for the tickets, so if we choose to take a brief detour, that's our right."

Yes, well, we still want to be courteous to the others in the group and not keep them waiting," said Dad. "We don't want to be disrespectful, they paid for their ticket too."

"Come along, Beau," strutted Grandma Helen confidently. "Let's go and see if we can't stir up a little more perturbation for our lovely morning tour host, I think we've given her enough of a break, don't you?"

"Oh, I am so on it, Grandma," he saluted her. "Lead the way."

CHAPTER NINETEEN

I don't think I've ever seen someone so happy to walk away from a group of people more than Elena did when she was saying goodbye to all of us. The woman looked as though she could use a stiff drink (or three), and it had only just barely hit noon. Of course, I think what really ended up throwing her over the edge was when Grandma Helen and Beau decided to play Marco Polo (thankfully with their eyes open) around the courtyard of the House of the Vestal Virgins just before the tour had ended. The murderous look that came over Elena's face was definitely one for the record books, so it was honestly no surprise to any of us when she quickly wrapped up and angrily stomped away.

"I have never been so embarrassed in my life," said Mom. "I cannot believe the two of you made such spectacles of yourselves."

"Is it really that unbelievable?" asked Ezra. "I mean, I knew what we were in for the minute they both started yodeling at Flavian's Palace."

"Oh, dear God, don't remind me," she shuddered. "That was beyond mortifying."

"Okay, you have to admit the acoustics in some of those archways were pretty impressive, even the happy Hooters duo thought so," said Beau. "You know, for such a substantial man, I was surprised at all the high notes he was able to hit, I think he would make a wonderful tenor."

"Darling, that woman deserved it," said Grandma Helen. "Beau and I would never have done such things if she hadn't been so stern and unyielding throughout the entirety of the tour. I understand wanting to keep some semblance of control over a group of people, but to do it in such a deprecating and ridiculing way, well, that is inexcusable."

"Yeah, Mom, she even got mad at me for asking to go to the bathroom," said Beau. "It only took me 30 seconds to run in and out, and she still wasn't happy."

"Please tell me you at least made time to wash your hands," said Dad.

"I did, but there wasn't any soap," he shrugged.

"Okay, I'll admit she could have been a lot nicer about things, but that still doesn't give the two of you the right to act like little heathens," said Mom.

"Well, we're certainly not going to be able to book with them again, that's for sure," said Dad.

"Would you even want to?" asked Aunt Christine. "I hate to say it, but that woman seriously needs to relax, she's a tour guide for God's sake, not a member of the Carabinieri."

"Alright, listen," said Mom. "I fully expect the two of you to be on your best behavior during this afternoon's tour; there will be no yodeling, childish games, or interruptions of any kind, do we have an understanding?"

"Yes," they nodded obediently.

"Good, now let's just pray we don't have her for this afternoon's tour," she said. "I'm fairly certain she'd cancel on the spot the minute she saw us coming."

"Or have a coronary," said Beau.

Thankfully, Elena did not show up to lead our next tour, and we were actually able to breathe a little bit easier as Marco, a jovial and vivacious man, took us on a guided tour through ancient subterranean Catacombs and the underground ossuary of the Capuchin Crypts.

We started by boarding a small shuttle bus that drove us directly outside the city walls and over to one of the forty ancient underground catacombs currently open to the public. These subterranean tombs had allowed Jewish and Christian Roman citizens to bury their dead without fear of being punished, and since Christians did not agree with the pagan custom of cremation (and because Roman law prohibited any type of burial within the interior of the city) underground catacombs quickly became a popular alternative.

As we walked through the long and narrow subterranean passageways, we found ourselves encased in an underground labyrinth of excavated graves, each one a stark representation of the trials and tribulations faced by early Christians who had simply wanted to honor their faith and preserve their place in Heaven. Despite the many challenges, the more than 92 miles of underground burial systems provided peace and hope for Christians as they were able to bury their dead using Christian symbols without fear of any kind of persecution.

The second half of the tour consisted of a visit to the Capuchin Crypt, a museum that houses five chapels beneath the Church of Santa Maria, each decorated in the bones, skulls, and complete skeletal remains of 3700 Capuchin friars believed to have died between 1528 and 1870. Each chapel's walls and ceilings are completely covered in human bones and showcase chandeliers made from vertebrae, arches made from skulls, and multiple "decorative" mosaics made with a variety of skeletal remains. There are even entire skeletons dressed in hooded monk robes lurking in the corners of a few of the rooms, which if I'm being completely honest, was more than a little disturbing.

Marco insists that the display is not in any way meant to be grisly, but rather a silent reminder that death happens to us all. The Capuchins believed that eternal life awaited for all who embraced and accepted Christ, so the intention of the display was primarily to help people celebrate death, not fear it.

"Now this is cool!" said Beau, taking in the macabre sight. "I mean, if Jeffery Dahmer had a lair, I bet it would look exactly like this, minus the religious part, of course."

"Once again, Beau, your ability to connect the reverent to the repellent is truly astounding," said Dad. "You make your mother and me so proud."

"Hey, I just call it like I see it," he shrugged. "You have to agree, though, the connection between the two kind of makes sense."

"What connection?" asked Mom, joining them in the first chapel.

"Trust me, you'd rather not know," said Dad.

As the rest of us made our way into the chapel area, Grandma Helen gasped in astonishment, "Oh dear God, as if that dark, dank labyrinth of death wasn't enough, now you want me to look at hanging dismembered dead people, I thought this was supposed to be part of a church, not a mass grave."

"Signore, I know that all of this may seem a bit gruesome," said Marco. "But you must understand that it was originally created to remind people of the transient nature of human life, that death comes for us all, and that time is fleeting." He pointed to a plaque on the wall, "In fact, that inscription up there was inspired by an old Roman proverb that says, 'Memento mori' which means, 'Remember you must die.'"

"Finally, a thought to raise all of our spirits," she snarked. Thank you for that, Marco."

Beau read over another sign written in Latin and began translating aloud, "What you are now, we once were; what we are now, you shall be."

"You read Latin?" asked Marco.

"I dabble," shrugged Beau.

"130Amiliar130e voi siete noi eravmo, 130amiliar130e noi siamo voi sarete," said Marco excitedly. "It's so interesting to know that you study Latin, I wish more young people would take the time to learn it."

"It's not by choice, Marco, believe me," said Beau. "My mother loves to drill it into my head daily even though she knows I'd really rather be learning Russian."

Seeing the look of confusion wash over his face, Mom quickly intervened, "We homeschool and Latin just so happens to be one of his subjects."

"Oh, I see," he smiled. "Well, knowing Latin will help you learn many other languages, perhaps not Russian, but definitely many of the different Romance languages that have been derived from Vulgar Latin."

"Vulgar, as in bad words?" asked Beau. "Hey Mom, how come you've never taught me any of that?"

"Not vulgar as in 'offensive' or 'rude,' honey," she clarified. "It was the type of Latin spoken primarily by the common middle class within the Roman Empire."

"And just like that, I'm back to hating Latin again," he said.

"Well, if you'll excuse me," said Marco. "I think I'll go and see if anyone else requires my assistance."

"Ugh, please tell me it's almost over," groaned Grandma Helen. "I don't think I can take much more of this."

"Not to worry, Mother, this is the final dreg of the tour," said Mom. "Your brief foray into erudition will soon be coming to a close, so you can now rest easy."

"Oh goody!" she clapped her hands giddily. "I say we all go and celebrate with an Aperol Spritz."

"I'm definitely on board with that idea," said Aunt Christine, raising her hand. "I think I've had more than my fill of death and decay for the afternoon."

"Yeah, Mom, this is really creepy," I said.

"Addie's right, it's creepier than a backrub from Grandma," said Ezra, walking up behind me. "And the fact that it sits directly under a church is even more disturbing."

"Were neither of you listening when Marco explained the significance of all of this and what it really means?" she asked bewilderedly. "The man literally spent ten minutes apprising us of the situation so that we would keep our judgements in check and approach all of this with an open mind."

"Mom, you've always told us that just because we have an idea, it doesn't necessarily mean that it should be brought to fruition." He pointed to the ceiling above, "Nailing the skeletal remains of a child to the roof, along with a scale and death sickle in each hand, does not strike me as a good idea, it's aberrant and completely unnatural."

She slowly looked up to where he was pointing and then quickly turned on her heel, "You're right, I think we've seen enough for the day, let's get out of here."

The rest of the day was spent enjoying the many different sights of Rome. We were able to see the Pantheon, Trevi Fountain, and Piazza Navona, as well as a few smaller archaeological digs that were currently underway. Known as the Eternal City, Rome has become the perfect blend of the ancient and the modern in that it glorifies all elements of history while integrating an urban landscape that not only compliments the agelessness of the city but also embraces its antiquity.

After dinner we decided to head back to the hotel for a few late-night drinks up at the rooftop bar. As we exited the elevator, we were immediately greeted by a young woman standing just outside the bar area.

"Bonasera," she smiled. "Will you be dining with us this evening?"

"Actually, we were just hoping to have a drink or two in the bar, if that's alright," said Grandpa Anthony. "Should we have made a reservation?"

"Oh no, Signore," she smiled. "We have plenty of room at the bar, just let me push a few tables together and I'll be right back."

After the hostess seated us, we ordered our drinks, and then gazed out at the breathtaking view of the Colosseum, its subtle nighttime lighting casting a soft glow across its famous archways.

"Wow, look at that view," said Aunt Christine. "Lorenzo was right, it's absolutely gorgeous up here."

"I really wish we were able to stay here for a few more days," I sighed. "There's just so much to see and do here, I hardly think we've even begun to scratch the surface."

"Yes, well, I'm ready to go," said Grandma Helen. "I've had entirely too much history and death; these grungy and dilapidated buildings are beginning to make my skin crawl."

"Let me get this straight, you're telling me that the historical ruins of a populace that practically laid the groundwork for all modern architecture, technology, language, and art make your skin crawl?" said Mom. "What is wrong with you?"

"Have you got an hour?" snarked Beau quietly.

"I like clean spaces, Olivia, you know this about me," she said. "Much of what we saw today was so antiquated and run down; you may like things like that, dear, but I do not."

"It's true, honey," said Grandpa Anthony. "Not everyone has your penchant for history and archaeological discovery." He then put his arm around Grandma Helen, "I'm proud of you, sweetheart, you stuck with us today and I know that wasn't easy for you."

Just then a loud voice boomed out from the corner of the room, "Bonasera!" yelled a young hip DJ into his microphone, "You know, I think it's time we take this night up to the next level, so let's get started!"

"No, that isn't necessary, dear," called out Grandma Helen. "We've only just received our drinks, so maybe you could just hold off a bit longer before starting."

The DJ either didn't hear her or chose to ignore her completely because he immediately started playing loud pulsating music that literally vibrated its way up through the legs of our chairs and into our bodies.

"I believe that would be an Italian 'no' Grandma," yelled Ezra. He took a sip of his beer and then smiled over at me, "So, how long do you think she'll last?"

"I can't imagine very long," I said. "Techno's not necessarily her speed.

132

"Five bucks says she'll finish her drink," said Beau. "Grandma's never been a quitter."

"Okay, I'll take that bet," laughed Ezra.

As the music pulsated, two very drunk and scantily clad middle-aged women stood up and began gyrating unabashedly to the music. As they erotically cavorted in front of the DJ, they flirted with two older gentlemen who had become completely entranced by the provocative display before them.

"I thought this was supposed to be a garden bar," yelled Mom over the music. "I don't really think this music vibes very well with the hotel's core clientele, do you?"

"Well it would seem that our two resident ecdysiasts, Tiffany and Tickle, would disagree with that assessment," said Grandma Helen, finishing her drink.

"What's an ecdysiast?" asked Beau.

"A stripper," answered Mom.

"Oh, okay," he nodded in understanding. He leaned in and yelled across the table, "I suppose that makes sense since you can see their thongs every time they bend over."

As we turned our attention over to the two women on the floor, Mom immediately tossed back the rest of her drink and then shouted out, "Okay, time to go!"

CHAPTER TWENTY

"If I didn't know any better, I'd think we were in some trash-infested slum," sneered Grandma Helen. "I'm honestly surprised some poor adolescent boy hasn't already jumped out of the corner of an alleyway to spray the car windows for money."

"It's raining, Grandma, even the most astute window-washer knows his limitations," said Ezra.

"Well, I just never expected Naples to look like this," she said. "It's so filthy and unsightly, thank God we don't have to spend more than an hour here."

We had only just arrived in Naples and were currently en route to the ferry dock where we would board the ferry that would take us over to Positano. Thankfully we had the presence of mind to book a private car because the anarchy witnessed at the taxi stand outside the train station was unbelievable. Three rows of cabs, each with at least fifteen cars, honking their horns incessantly trying to get the lines to move faster. Cab drivers yelled out their windows telling the drivers at the front of the line to hurry up, while others shouted directly at the patrons, themselves, willing them to get their luggage loaded quickly. It was a complete madhouse, and all of the honking, yelling, and cursing did nothing more than create further chaos, it was pandemonium at its finest, and I was glad to be able to escape it.

"Can you believe how crazy that taxi stand was?" asked Aunt Christine. "I don't think I've ever seen anything like it."

"And those cab drivers yelling at all those people to get a move on with their luggage, I mean, how rude and insensitive can you be?" said Mom. "It's a train station for God's sake, people are going to have luggage."

"Imagine what they would have done had they seen us coming with all of Grandma's luggage," said Ezra. "We would've been lynched on the spot."

As we continued to discuss the craziness of the taxi stand, our own personal driver carefully pulled over and stopped the car.

"Uh, scusa," he said, pointing out the front window. "Too much traffic, you can walk from here, yes?"

"Have you lost your mind," exclaimed Grandma Helen. "It's raining, of course, we can't walk from here."

"Uh, what seems to be the problem, Tony," interjected Grandpa Anthony diplomatically.

"I'm so sorry, signore, but I cannot cross" he gestured out the window again. "It's going to be difficult with all of this traffic and will be much faster if you walk; you may miss your ferry if you don't."

"But it's raining!" reiterated Grandma Helen indignantly. "My hair will be ruined."

"I'm sorry, signora, but I cannot cross," he said defensively. "The rain is causing delays."

"We completely understand, Tony, thank you," said Grandpa Anthony. He then turned and patted her knee calmly, "Honey, you'll be fine, you have a hood on the back of your coat, so that should keep you relatively dry; it's not but a five-minute walk from here."

"But hoods flatten my hair, Anthony, you know this!" she protested.

"Just put the damn hood on, Mother," whispered Mom into her ear. "I have no plans to miss the ferry on account of your vanity."

"Ugh, fine," she relented. "But we had better be getting a portion of our money back for this, I didn't pay out the nose to walk in the rain."

As Dad, Grandpa Anthony, and Ezra unloaded the luggage from the back of the car, Grandma Helen stepped out from the passenger's side and immediately let out a high-pitched scream.

"Mom!" yelled Mom toppling out after her. "Are you okay?"

"Olivia," she pointed down at the ground. "What is that, exactly?"

"Jesus, Mom, I thought you were hurt," she said, relief washing over her. "I hate when you do that to me!"

"I'm sorry, dear, I didn't mean to alarm you," she said penitently. "But is that what I think it is?"

"Oh, dear God, I think it is," said Mom disgustedly. "Okay, let's just get away from it."

"What's wrong?" asked Aunt Christine. "Mom, are you okay?"

"I was fine until I almost stepped into that giant pile of human excrement on the street," she said. "Whoever would do something so revolting and abhorrent?"

"Apparently someone incredibly bold," said Beau, looking over her shoulder. "And if I'm not mistaken, someone who has also recently eaten a good bit of corn."

"Ew, God, you are so disgusting, Beau!" I yelled out. "I can't believe you even looked closely enough to notice something like that."

"Hey, I can't help it if I have 20/20 vision," he snapped back. "Besides, I'm not the one who left the digested remnants of last night's dinner out on the street for all to see, so shut up!"

"Okay, both of you please stop," said Mom. "Standing here in the rain yelling at each other is not making any of this go away, so let's just make our way over to the ferry dock and forget that the last 45 minutes even happened."

"Fine by me," said Grandma Helen. "I've had about as much of Naples as I can take; this place is loathsome."

"Is everything okay, what's going on?" asked Dad. He immediately glanced down at the pile of excrement, "Is that…"

"Yes," we said in unison.

"Well, I can honestly say I wasn't expecting to see something like that today," he said calmly.

"Yeah, Naples has been a real treat," drawled Beau.

"Alright, let's just get ourselves to the ferry," said Dad. "And whatever you do, watch where you step, we have no idea if this is common practice, so it's better to be safe than sorry."

"Okay, people, it's time to play dodge the biohazard," exclaimed Beau. "We don't want anyone dying on us before we get to Positano."

"Ugh, I absolutely hate it here, Olivia," shuddered Grandma Helen. "I'm in desperate need of a drink, a valium, or both."

"We'll see what we can do for you, Mom," she said, placing an arm around her.

It took us about ten minutes to cross through the jumble of traffic and over to the marina, but we were able to make it onto the ferry with a few minutes to spare. The upper level had been closed off, which limited available seating, but thankfully we were able to find a group of seats toward the stern of the boat. In the center of the room stood a large concession stand offering various coffee drinks, sodas, and snacks, so of course, Beau made an immediate beeline over to the man standing behind the counter, with me, Mom, and Grandma Helen following close behind.

"Hello, can I please get six cappuccinos, one Coke, and…" she glanced briefly over at Grandma Helen, "Mom, what do you want?"

"I don't suppose you have any vodka back there," she sighed.

"Uh, no, signora," he shook his head. "I'm sorry, I do not."

"What about something that will erase the last harrowing hour from my memory?" she said. "I'll honestly take anything with alcohol at this point."

"Scusi?" he said.

"Okay, that's enough, Mother," said Mom. "Either order something or walk away."

"Ugh, fine, I suppose I'll have a cappuccino as well, then," she groaned. She pulled a few napkins from a dispenser, "I just want to get to Positano and forget that Naples even exists; I simply don't understand how people can even live here, it's absolutely horrid."

"Well, I can't say I disagree with you, Grandma," said Beau, twisting open his soda. "Having to hopscotch over freshly laid dung grenades has made me realize that Naples is definitely not for me." He took a sip of his drink and shrugged casually, "I suppose that means San Francisco's out too."

We thanked the man at the concession stand and then walked back over to our seats where Grandpa Anthony was laying out the agenda for the next few days.

"Okay, so day one has us at a small intimate cooking class at La Tagliata at 12:00, day two is going to be spent at the beach, day three will be a private boat tour up along the coast, and day four is going to be entirely free except for the dinner at the restaurant Jack reserved for us."

"Ugh, don't remind me," snarled Grandma Helen. "I feel dirty even talking about it."

"Don't start, Mom," warned Aunt Christine. "It's simply a friendly gesture, that's all."

"Yes, and John Wayne Gacy was simply a children's party clown," she mumbled. "And we all know what happened there."

"This is really eating you up, isn't it, Grandma?" said Ezra quietly.

"Like a carnivorous bacteria," she curled her lip.

"Look, I'm sure Aunt Christine knows what she's doing," he said. "She's been burned by him before; she won't allow him to do it again."

"I pray, you're right, dear," she smiled wanly. "I'm well aware that she doesn't want to be romantically involved with Jack, but she's always been so gullible wherever he's concerned, I'm just afraid he's going to hurt her in other ways, that's all."

"I honestly think he's just trying to make up for past mistakes," soothed Ezra. "He knows Aunt Christine's happy now, he's not going to try to ruin that for her."

"That man is not the magnanimous type, Ezra, I know he's up to something," she said. "I just don't know what."

The ferry ride had taken a little over an hour, so by the time we were pulling into port, the rain had stopped and the sun was shining. We walked outside and stood under the covered portion of the stern watching the scenic town of Positano come into view. Situated along the Amalfi Coast, this little romantic city is known for the many colorful houses that vertically rest upon the cliffsides overlooking the Tyrrhenian Sea. The city gained a great deal of notoriety back in the 1950's when it first garnered favor amongst the literary and artistic elite, however since then it has grown into an immensely popular tourist area boasting multiple restaurants, bars, and high-end boutiques that happily cater to the throngs of vacationers visiting each year.

"Did you know that there are more than 10,000 steps in and around the town of Positano, isn't that completely mind-boggling?" I asked.

"Ugh, I can already feel my knees aching," said Mom. "Thankfully I packed plenty of ibuprofen for this portion of the trip."

"Not to worry, dear," said Grandma Helen, patting her hand. "Your father was able to find us a lovely hotel right by the water, so climbing up and down those stairs won't present a problem."

"I'm sorry, have we decided to not visit the upper portion of the city?" asked Mom. "Or even the middle portion, for that matter?"

"Don't be daft, Olivia, of course, we will," she snickered. "We'll just take a cab whenever we do."

"Mom, that's going to get costly," she said. "I can see you and Dad taking one, but as for the rest of us, we should be fine."

"Suit yourself," she shrugged. "Personally, I wouldn't willingly put myself in a situation where I might die, but then again, you've always been a risk-taker."

"Gee, thanks for the vote of confidence," said Mom. "I'm not knocking on death's door, you know, I'm actually in pretty good shape."

"Yes, of course, you are, dear," she smiled. "But you're also no spring chicken either, so you may want to keep that in mind as you stroll around these treacherous hills; parents are expected to leave this world before their children, not after, and I'm not prepared to have you go before me, darling."

As Mom stood there in stunned silence, one of the ferrymen called out loudly, "Positano!"

"Ooh, there disembarking, time to go!" beamed Grandma Helen.

"Everything okay?" asked Dad, walking up beside her.

"You mean other than my Mother insinuating that I'm older than God and might die if I take more than ten vertical steps up one of those hills," she asked. "Yeah, everything's fine."

"You're at the prime of your life honey, don't listen to your mother," he said. "Besides, I still find you incredibly sexy." He put his arms around her and nuzzled her neck, "In fact, why don't I show you how sexy I think you are later tonight."

"Ew, gross," said Beau, as he walked by. "There better not be any of that going on in the room tonight, I'd really rather not have to vomit in my bed."

"What is he talking about?" asked Dad bewildered.

"Um, I think I may have forgotten to mention that Dad was only able to book two rooms instead of four," said Mom uneasily. "So, Beau and Ezra will be staying in our room."

"Please tell me you're joking," he said.

"I wish I was," she sighed. "Look, it's only for a few nights, and from what I understand, each room has a balcony with an ocean view, so you'll be able to smoke your pipe in the evenings without anyone disturbing you."

"I'm sorry, have you even met our children?" he raised his brow. He adjusted the strap of the bag hanging off his shoulder, "Well, I suppose it's better than having to room with your mother again, that was definitely one for the record books."

As we stood in line waiting for the ferry ramp to lower, we could hear the loud hum of a speed boat quickly approaching, its drivers, two swarthy-looking men smiling gleefully as they drove a group of a young vivacious blond women out to sea.

"Hey Dad," shouted Beau unabashedly, "I think you're right; the Somali pirates did expand their network."

Mom, whose face had become completely flushed with embarrassment, turned directly toward Dad with a murderous look in her eye, "I'm going to kill you, Greg."

CHAPTER TWENTY-ONE

The next morning, Aunt Christine, Grandma Helen, and I were sitting on the hotel terrace having breakfast when Mom unceremoniously plopped down at the table, picked up a fork, and began stabbing at the few slices of kiwi left on my plate.

"Please tell me this isn't a buffet," she said, her mouth full of kiwi. "I just don't think my body can handle that right now and I really need someone to serve me."

"There's a woman that comes by to take coffee and drink orders," I said. But the pastries, cereal, and everything else are actually inside the restaurant."

"What's going on with you?" asked Aunt Christine.

"Ugh, I hurt," groaned Mom. She popped a few ibuprofen into her mouth and swallowed them down with water, "This is definitely a young person's city, my knees are absolutely killing me."

"A tad bit sore, are we, dear?" asked Grandma Helen raising her brow.

"Unfortunately, yes," she said. "Greg and I decided to check out that wine bar up on Viale Pasitea last night but had no idea we'd have to hurdle ourselves through the Olympic steeplechase to get there; my legs felt like jelly afterward and I'm barely able to move this morning."

"Well..." she started.

"Don't even say it, Mother," said Mom, cutting her off. "My body is saying plenty, I don't need you adding your two cents."

"I was simply going to say that a mimosa might help rejuvenate you a bit, darling, that's all," she replied, taking a sip of coffee, "Of course, I did try warning you that this was going to happen, but I'm not going to tell you 'I told you so,' even though I really did."

"I believe that's exactly what you're doing, Mother," said Mom sourly.

"Well, it's certainly not intentional, dear," she chirped happily. "It just happened to slip out."

"Hey, why don't I go and fix you a plate," said Aunt Christine, rising from her chair. "I know exactly how you're feeling right now, I felt the same way after I went skiing with Brian last year; I strained muscles I didn't even know I had."

"You sure it was just from the skiing?" asked Mom, giving her a wry smile.

"Get your mind out of the gutter, Ollie," laughed Aunt Christine. She turned to leave and then slyly spoke over her shoulder, "And no, it wasn't just from the skiing, there were many other extracurricular activities at play that weekend."

"I knew it," chuckled Mom, stealing a strawberry from my plate. "Honestly though, it's as if my mind still thinks I'm 25, while my body acts as if I died during the Korean War." She quickly ate the strawberry and added, "Age definitely has a way of creeping up on you, that's for sure."

"And let's not forget about menopause, dear," said Grandma Helen. "That always seems to be the gift that keeps on giving, even after one becomes postmenopausal."

"Ugh, don't remind me," she said. "I'm so sick of having to deal with all these hot flashes and everything else that comes along with it, I'm just ready to be done with it all."

"Wait a minute," I said. "I thought menopause was just the ending of your period and a few years of hot flashes, you're telling me there's more?"

They both burst out in uproarious laughter.

"Oh, honey, that's only the beginning," said Mom. "There's also hormone fluctuations, night sweats, sleep deprivation, exhaustion, heart palpitations—"

"Buongiorno," interjected a voice from behind me. "Would you care for something to drink?"

"May I suggest a round of mimosas, dear,'" said Grandma Helen.

"Yes, definitely," said Mom. "And a cappuccino, I am in desperate need of caffeine as well."

"I'll take a mimosa too, please, if you don't mind," said Aunt Christine, setting down a plate in front of Mom.

"Yes, of course, signora," said the server. "I'll be back soon."

"I wasn't really sure what you wanted so I just got you a smattering of everything," said Aunt Christine.

"Thanks, Chrissy," said Mom gratefully. She took a bite out of a croissant and sighed contentedly, "Wow, it really is beautiful here, isn't it?"

We had been enjoying our morning out on the terrace, an enchanting space that invoked a sense of peace and tranquility similar to that found in the glistening and placid waters of the Mediterranean below. The balcony's railings had been completely covered in a variety of multi-colored flower boxes, each one overflowing with radiant blooms, while a bougainvillea-covered pergola roof hung high above to provide plenty of shade from the late morning sun. It was the quintessential Mediterranean-inspired rooftop, complete with flowy white linen curtains, lemon-themed ceramic tiles, and wrought-iron tables decorated in yellow and blue napery.

"Look, all I'm saying is that if you really want to test the depth of your love for another person, come to Europe and spend at least a week sharing a bathroom with them," said Beau, taking a seat next to me. "You may actually find that you're not as lucky in love as you originally thought."

Beau and Ezra had just come downstairs to join us for breakfast, and as usual, Beau was already running his mouth about things he knew nothing about.

"What are you even talking about?" I asked.

"Dr. Ruth over here was telling me that if I want to test the threshold of my relationship with Sabrina, I should really think about bringing her to Europe to see how we handle sharing a small bathroom with no ventilation system," answered Ezra. "That, apparently, will be the true test of our love for one another."

"Hey, I'm serious, there is no truer testament of love than that," stated Beau firmly. "Take Mom and Dad for example—"

"Oh, no you don't," interjected Mom. "I have no desire to hear any of your theories on my relationship with your father, thank you very much."

"It's not a bad thing, Mom, I swear," he said defensively. He reached over and grabbed a half-eaten croissant off Mom's plate, "Remember last night when you went into the bathroom just as Dad was coming out?"

"Yes, what about it?" she answered.

"Well, you didn't even flinch, you just walked right in as if it were nothing, even though you and I both know the man's been eating entirely too much shellfish lately. That right there is a true testament of love; I mean, you couldn't have paid me enough to enter that tiny unventilated space after him, and yet, you just charged right on in and didn't even think twice about it."

"Beau, I've been married to him for close to 24 years, nothing really shocks me anymore," she said. "Besides, I've actually grown used to it."

"Grown used to what?" asked Dad.

He and Grandpa Anthony had just come from the buffet table and were walking over to take their seats.

"Oh, nothing," smiled Mom. "Beau was just regaling us with his theory on what makes a relationship work, and apparently ours works because I'm not afraid to use the bathroom immediately after you."

"Makes sense, I suppose," he shrugged. "Lord knows I've had to follow after you plenty of times, and if I can survive something like that, I can survive anything."

"Gregory Jenkins!" yelled Mom, throwing her napkin at him. "You take that back right now!"

"Oh relax, honey, I'm only joking," he said. "Although I do see your point, Beau, something like that could quite possibly make or break a relationship. Thankfully your Mother's love for me is beyond such pettiness; God has truly blessed me."

"Laying it on a bit thick there, Dad, don't you think?" drawled Ezra.

"Nope, not at all, son," he smiled. "You see, the true key to any relationship is knowing when to speak and knowing when to keep your mouth shut, and since the latter always seems to be a bit more difficult, I find it best to make the former as laudatory as possible."

"You are so full of it, Greg," laughed Mom.

"I know, but it sounded good and that's all that really matters," he winked.

***

144

After breakfast, we walked over to La Tagliata for our afternoon cooking class. The restaurant was literally a stone's throw away from our hotel, so thankfully there was no need to climb an inordinate amount of stairs to get there. As we walked through the door, we were immediately greeted by a young gentleman standing behind a tall wooden podium.

"Buon pomeriggio, welcome to La Tagliata," he said. "Are you the Vitali's, by any chance?"

"Yes, I'm Anthony Vitalli" answered Grandpa Anthony. "I believe we have a reservation for an afternoon cooking class with Serafina at 12:00."

"Si, si," said the man, nodding his head. "Uh, I am so sorry, but Serafina has had a…um…a, how do you say, emergenza f145amiliare, and cannot be here today."

"A what?" asked Ezra.

"A family emergency," said Grandpa Anthony.

"Oh, parli Italiano?" said the man with a hopeful look in his eyes.

"Si," he nodded.

Upon confirmation that Grandpa Anthony could understand him, he immediately began speaking rapidly in Italian, his arms flailing about as he did. As the two of them conversed back and forth, the rest of us could only sit back and watch as we were unable to understand anything that was being said. As soon as the man had finished talking, he held up a finger indicating that we should wait and then headed toward the back of the restaurant.

"What was that all about?" asked Grandma Helen.

"Apparently, Serafina's daughter broke her arm at school today and she had to leave early to take her to the hospital, so she won't be able to teach our class," he answered. "However, Dante, that's his name by the way, has invited us to join him upstairs for his class, but he says that it's slightly different than what we were supposed to do with Serafina."

"Different, how?" asked Mom.

"Well, apparently the one we signed up for takes place downstairs in the back of the kitchen where they hold their smaller and more intimate classes," he said. "The one upstairs is going to be larger, louder, and a bit more lively."

"Oh, well, that shouldn't be a problem," said Mom. "It sounds like it'll be fun."

"Said the woman who giddily spent two hours playing with her new packing cubes," said Aunt Christine.

"Okay, that's not fair," said Mom. "Even you were impressed with how much I was able to fit into those things."

Just then, Dante came back and handed each of us a wine-themed apron before beckoning us to follow him upstairs. As we reached the upper level, we discovered that it was actually a covered terrace over-looking the water, and though it wasn't a large space, it was more than enough to accommodate the twenty of us who were in attendance.

At the center of the room stood an incredibly long metal table with multiple bowls, plates, cooking utensils, and electric mixers set up in separate personal stations. Wooden chairs were lined up behind both sides of the table and there was a large black buffet in the corner holding at least twenty different bottles of open wine.

"Well, this certainly seems to be starting out well," said Aunt Christine admiring the view. "Three hours up here will definitely be time well spent."

"Wow, that view is absolutely amazing," I said.

"And look at all of that wine," said Grandma Helen, her eyes dancing with delight. "They even have the Santa Margherita Prosecco I love so much; oh this is going to be great!"

As we made our way over to the empty workstations, Dante quickly filled everyone's wine glasses and encouraged us to introduce ourselves as he quietly went to work preparing the ingredients that would be needed for the first course. Another man named Antonio eventually came out to help and together they began teaching us how to make gnocchi, a small potato dumpling that has become quite popular in Italian cuisine. As Dante and Antonio showed us how to carefully knead the dough, I could faintly hear the soft melody of music playing in the background. About ten minutes later, with the dough cut into smaller bite-sized pieces, another staff member came upstairs and took the gnocchi back down to the kitchen where it would eventually be boiled in water and then topped with a decadent homemade tomato cream sauce and fresh parmigiana.

With the wine flowing freely, it was easy to see that everyone was beginning to loosen up a bit. The music seemed livelier and the group as a whole appeared to be much more relaxed. The next recipe to be introduced was tiramisu, and as soon as Dante and Antonio added all of the ingredients into each of our bowls, they encouraged everyone to dance and sing while mixing it all together. Grandma Helen, who was completely in her element at this point, was having an absolute blast as she happily gyrated to the boisterous music that was now blaring from the speakers.

"Oh, this is so much fun!" she yelled out. "Look at my tiramisu, isn't it coming along beautifully?" She downed the wine in her glass and held it up exuberantly, "Dante, more vino!"

"Uh, is Grandma already drunk, she seems to be just a wee bit out of control," I said.

"Oh God, no," said Mom, shaking her head. "This just happens to be her natural comportment anytime wine and celebration come together; we've decided to find it charming."

"Olivia, darling, can you please help me pour this final layer over my ladyfingers?" asked Grandma Helen. "My wrist is hurting and it's hard for me to hold the bowl and scoop it all out."

"Yes, of course," she said, taking the bowl from her hands.

"But don't sprinkle the cocoa powder on it," she added quickly. "I want to be the one to do that."

"I'll be sure to restrain myself from reaching for the shaker," said Mom rolling her eyes.

Once the tiramisu was finished and placed in the refrigerator to set, Dante and Antonio immediately began teaching us how to make eggplant parmesan. Of course, this is where things really began getting exciting as eggplants were starting to be tossed around the table just as the lively rhythm of disco music began to fill the room; and since disco speaks directly to Grandma Helen's soul, it was honestly no surprise to find her immediately ditching her workstation to sing and dance around the entire table as soon as Gloria Gaynor's *I Will Survive* started to play. In fact, Dante and Antonio were so mesmerized by her performance, that they quickly helped her up onto a chair so that she could have a makeshift stage to sing her little heart out on.

Everyone was clapping and cheering, some were even whistling while twirling their white napkins high above their heads urging her to keep singing; she was definitely in her element and these people were eating it up. As the song began to wind down, Dante and Antonio immediately helped her down from the chair and she happily sauntered her way back over to her workstation.

"Oh, I do so love impromptu performances," she said gleefully. "It makes me miss being on stage and in front of an audience." She started to slice the eggplant in front of her, "You know, I think we should try to find—"

"No," said Mom, shaking her head emphatically.

"What are you a cocktail?" she snapped. "Don't shake your head at me."

"Mother, none of us are interested in doing what you're wanting to do," said Mom.

"You don't even know what I was going to say," she said indignantly.

Mom looked sardonically over at her, "Hmm, let's see, the thrill of the crowd was completely intoxicating and now you want to find a place to sing karaoke so that your ego can be fed a little bit more, do I have that about right?"

"No, actually, you don't," she answered haughtily.

"Oh, and where did I go wrong, exactly?" asked Mom, raising her brow.

"Well, it was really more exhilarating than intoxicating and…" she paused momentarily before adding irritably, "Oh, stop gloating, Olivia, it doesn't become you."

Chapter Twenty-Two

Our third day in Positano was spent doing absolutely nothing other than enjoying a lazy day at the beach. Grandma Helen had decided to stay behind at the hotel to visit the day spa, while the rest of us ventured out to savor a beautiful afternoon by the water. After a few hours, Mom, Dad, and Aunt Christine decided it was time to get out from the sun, so they walked over to the elevated ocean bar behind us for a few seaside cocktails, while Beau, Ezra, Grandpa Anthony, and I opted to stay in our oceanfront loungers for a little while longer.

I had just returned from a refreshing swim when I immediately noticed that Beau had helped himself to the last half of my ham and cheese panini.

"Oh my gosh, Beau, you're such a pig!" I yelled. "I can't believe you ate the last of my sandwich."

"How do you know it was even me?" he asked innocently. "I'm not the only one sitting here, you know."

"I looked over at Ezra who was out for the count and snoring heavily, "I'm fairly certain Sleeping Beauty over here hasn't woken up in the last hour, so you tell me."

"Okay, fine, I was hungry, so sue me," he shrugged nonchalantly.

"That was my lunch you little twerp," I said. "And now it's completely gone, thanks to you."

He casually read the time on his phone, "Well, lunch was a few hours ago, and since you were taking entirely too long to finish it, I just decided to help you." He took a sip of water, "You're welcome, by the way."

"I can't believe you," I snarled. "You are so self-centered and gluttonous."

He looked me up and down in my pink and blue striped bikini and curled his lip, "Yeah, well, at least I don't look like a gender reveal party; what with your matching pink beach bag and blue coverup thingy, it all looks so pretentious and obnoxious."

"No, you're obnoxious!" I snapped.

"Oh whatever shall I do?" mocked Beau, putting his hands on the side of his face. "Addie thinks I'm obnoxious."

"Well, she does make a valid point, dear, you do tend to be somewhat obnoxious at times," said Grandma Helen walking up behind us. "Now, can either of you tell me where your Grandfather is, I need to have a quick chat with him."

"I have no idea where he went, Grandma," said Beau. "I was busy eating a sandwich."

"And I was swimming, so I don't really know either," I said, slapping Beau upside the head.

"I think he's still sitting with that group over there," said Ezra groggily.

"And what group would that be, dear?" she asked.

"I don't know, they're over there to the left somewhere," he said. "I think they asked him to join them for a drink."

She looked over to where a large group of people were laughing and talking and waved her arm in the air. "Anthony, darling, I need to talk to you!"

"Okay, honey, I'll be right there," he waved back.

He slowly stood up, bid farewell to his friends, and then walked over to us, "How was your spa day, dear, was it as good as you thought it would be?"

"Oh, it was simply marvelous," she drawled. "Chiara and Isabella took such good care of me and pampered me so much that I feel like a brand-new woman. The oxygen facial alone was to die for and has made my skin look so hydrated and radiant that I'm practically glowing."

"It looks exactly like it did this morning at breakfast; I'm sorry, can anyone say placebo effect?" mumbled Beau.

"You look absolutely beautiful, my love," said Grandpa Anthony. He picked up a bottle of water, "Now, what is it that you wanted to discuss with me?"

"Oh, I wanted to tell you that I stopped by the concierge desk like you asked me to and confirmed our reservation for tomorrow's boat ride up the coast," she said. "They did change the time from 9:00 to 9:30, but I didn't think that would be a problem."

"Oh yeah, that sounds perfect," he smiled. "I'm just glad to hear they're not canceling on us."

"So, who are all those people you were talking to?" she asked. "New friends?"

"Oh, they're actually a group of neighbors from Wisconsin that are here on vacation," he said. "They're planning to go to Rome and Venice after they leave here, so their trip is really just beginning."

"Together?" she asked incredulously. "Oh my God, how many are there?"

"Uh, six couples, I believe," he said.

"And they actually chose to come here together?" she asked again.

"Well, they're all recent empty-nesters and decided it would be kind of fun to celebrate their newfound freedom here in Italy, so yeah, they decided to do it together," he nodded.

"Ugh, I can't even imagine spending more than ten minutes with any of our neighbors, let alone taking an entire vacation with them," she shuddered. "That sounds unimaginably awful."

"Hey, do y'all hear that?" asked Ezra, placing a hand behind his ear.

"Hear what, dear?" she said.

"The collective sigh of relief our entire neighborhood has literally just exhaled, it's faint, but I can definitely hear it," he snarked. "Maybe it's just me."

"Well, aren't you the witty one," she said sardonically.

"Oh, I'm just kidding, Grandma," he chuckled. "You know I love you, even if our neighbors don't."

Just then we could hear the grumblings of Dad, Mom, and Aunt Christine as they made their way over to us.

"I'm sorry, but that was absolutely ridiculous," said Dad angrily. "I cannot believe we just spent over two hundred euros on six drinks."

"I don't know what happened," said Aunty Christine. "The menus we looked at did not have those prices."

"Something's not adding up," said Mom. "There's no way that all three of us misread that menu."

"What happened?" asked Grandpa Anthony.

"Well, we decided to head up to that bar for a few drinks," said Mom pointing behind her, "but the prices listed on the menu were very different from the prices we ended up seeing on our check."

"They practically tripled when we got our bill," said Dad. "They claim it's because we chose to sit on the couches rather than at tables, but I'm pretty sure that's just a way to scam the tourists; there weren't any signs mentioning that anywhere."

"Did you happen to pay with your credit card?" asked Grandpa Anthony.

"I did, yes," nodded Dad.

"Okay, let me have your receipt," he said, reaching out his hand. "I'll take care of this."

Dad handed him the receipt and we watched as he walked directly over to the manager who was standing beside the bar. He immediately showed him the receipt, picked up a menu, and then proceeded to point back and forth between the two. A minute later, the manager walked over to a computer, tapped on the screen a few times, and printed out another slip of paper, which he promptly handed to Grandpa Anthony.

After shaking the man's hand, he turned and sauntered his way back over to us, "You should see a refund on your card within the next five to seven days."

"Are you serious?" asked Dad.

"Yes," he nodded, holding out the slip of paper. "He refunded the entire check and apologized for any inconvenience."

"Wow, what did you say to get him to do that?" asked Mom.

"Don't you worry about that, honey," he smiled. "It's handled, that's all you need to know."

"I find it best not to ask questions, dear," said Grandma Helen, leaning in close to Mom. "The man has a certain way of handling things and sometimes they can be a bit unconventional if you know what I mean."

"I'm not entirely sure that I do, but okay," said Mom uneasily.

"Alright everyone, we should probably go ahead and get cleaned up for dinner," said Grandpa Anthony. "We have a 7:00 reservation and I'd hate to be late."

As we began packing our things, Ezra glanced over at Beau and me and smiled wickedly, "I bet you anything Grandpa's inner Don Corleone just made an appearance at that bar."

"Yeah, he probably made him an offer he couldn't refuse," snickered Beau. "He's got that subtle but dangerous side to him, you know?"

"Both of you stop, you're being ridiculous," I scoffed. "Grandpa wouldn't hurt a fly."

"Yeah, well, it's always the unassuming ones you need to worry about," said Ezra. "Grandpa might be subtle, but he's also got connections with people I certainly wouldn't want to mess with."

"I hope it's members of the Cosa Nostra," said Beau. "Now, those guys are badass."

"They're also incredibly deadly and don't think twice about killing anyone that crosses them," I said pointedly. "In fact, they'd probably eliminate you in a heartbeat if they thought it might benefit them."

"Well, I never said they weren't without flaws," he mumbled.

***

The next morning, we made our way down to Marina Grande, Positano's main pier, to meet the captain of the boat, Nico, who would be taking us on our tour of the Amalfi Coast. He was an incredibly jovial and affable man, probably somewhere in his late fifties, whose skin was tan and leathery from years of spending time in the sun. He had a warm smile that reached his eyes and had an uncanny way of making everyone feel at ease, especially Grandma Helen after he told her that she wouldn't have to worry about taking off her shoes.

Once we were all settled in our seats, Nico started the boat's engine and we slowly began pulling out of port, leaving the colorful city of Positano behind. It was an absolutely beautiful day and the sun's rays were practically dancing off the water, making the soft waves of the Mediterranean shimmer as they gently undulated off into the distance. As we continued to make our way up the coast, Nico began filling us in on a lot of the local culture, telling us where the best restaurants and bars were located and where we could find the best seafood linguini in all of Amalfi. He even shared a little bit of dirt on some of the celebrity encounters he's had over the years, which of course, had Grandma Helen literally at the edge of her seat and hanging on every word.

As Nico continued to point out the smaller fishing villages and towns along the coastline, I started to notice quite a few tall square stone towers looming high along the edge of the cliffs.

"Excuse me, Nico," I said, "but do you happen to know what those large towers are used for?"

"Those are the Saracen Towers," he called out over the boat's engine. "They were once part of a defense system that covered much of the southern Italian coast during the Middle Ages and were used to protect the people from the Arab, Islamic, and pirate attacks taking place during that time."

"Oh wow," said Mom. "Are they still in use today?"

"No, not really," he shook his head. "Some have been restored and now serve as tourist attractions, while others have become private residences." He pointed to the one that we were slowly coming up to, "And then there are some, like the one up there, that have been purchased by private individuals that do absolutely nothing with them and don't even allow visitors to enter."

"Why wouldn't they do anything with them?" asked Beau. "I can't imagine they come cheap."

No, they are definitely not cheap," said Nico. "Buyers purchase them from the government and when they do nothing with them, it tends to anger the locals who feel that a piece of their history has been stolen from them for no good reason; it's all very sad."

"That is sad," agreed Mom. "Can you imagine how much history those things have seen over the years?"

"More than any of us can imagine, I'm sure," said Dad.

After making a brief stop to see the Fiordo Di Furore, a famous narrow inlet of secluded beach that lays directly between the steep rock faces of a giant fjord, we continued further along to a private alcove area where Dad, Beau, Ezra, and I immediately jumped in for a refreshing swim.

After about twenty minutes, we made our way back onto the boat and began toweling off as a small, motorized watercraft sidled up next to us. The driver, who cheerfully greeted us in Italian, handed Nico an enormous platter of fruit skewers, and then quickly waved goodbye as he sped off in the same direction that he had just come from.

"Compliments of Ristorante Da Giana," smiled Nico, carefully setting the platter down in front of us. "That is the restaurant you will be eating lunch at when we visit the town of Amalfi, so please, enjoy!"

"That is so nice of them," said Aunt Christine.

"Wow, this looks delicious," said Ezra.

"Now that's what I call high-style service, Nico, "said Beau grabbing a skewer.

"Nico, darling," cooed Grandma Helen. "Do you happen to have a bowl and a napkin I can use, I'm really not much for primitive eating."

"Uh, no, signora, I don't think that I do," he said. "But I can try and find one if you'd like."

"No, that's alright, Nico, we'll make this work," smiled Mom.

"But I don't like to eat skewered food, Olivia, you know this," she hissed. "It's not only boorish but incredibly uncouth."

"Listen, I honestly don't care whether you eat it or not," said Mom. "But I refuse to allow you to denigrate this man's kindness by being rude and catty, that too is uncouth."

"I am not at all being rude and cat-" she paused momentarily. "Wait a minute, are those champagne flutes I hear?"

"I don't hear anything," said Mom looking around.

"That's because you're too busy scolding me like I'm some sort of insolent child rather than a sophisticated adult who understands the importance of mannerliness and etiquette." She crossed her arms defiantly, "And I'll have you know that I do not appreciate it."

"Prosecco, anyone?" asked Nico, holding up a tray full of glasses.

"Ooh...Ooh, me first, me first!" yelled Grandma Helen, pushing Aunt Christine aside as she lunged for the tray.

CHAPTER TWENTY-THREE

"Are you almost ready, Mom?" asked Aunt Christine. "The limo's going to be here in about ten-minutes, so we probably need to start heading downstairs."

"Don't rush me, Christine, I said I'd be ready and I will be," she said, spritzing herself with perfume. "Why don't the three of you just head downstairs and I'll join you when I'm done."

"No, I don't think so," she said shaking her head. "You're ADHD-addled mind tends to go off of the rails sometimes and I really don't want to be late for our reservation. Jack went to a lot of trouble to set this up for us and I don't want to be rude by not showing up on time."

In honor of our last night in Positano, Jack had made a reservation for all of us at Il Fiore, a five-star restaurant owned by his good friend, Arturo, who he's apparently known for many years. The restaurant is located in Montepertuso, a small hamlet situated directly above the city of Positano, and since it's about a twenty-minute car ride away, Jack also took it upon himself to organize our transportation there.

"Don't you find it odd that he's having a limo pick us up?" I asked. "I mean, the hotel shuttle could have just taken us there for free."

"I think he just wanted to make our last night in Positano special," smiled Aunt Christine. "He's really trying to make this new friendship work, and for Jack, that usually means going above and beyond what's expected, even if it costs a lot of money."

"Well, I think it's pretentious, ostentatious, and completely unnecessary," snarled Grandma Helen. "And I can assure you it's not a simple friendship he's after."

"Okay, listen, had this been arranged by anyone else, you would be absolutely euphoric right now and you know it," said Mom. "You live to make an entrance."

"That may be true, dear, but it's not anyone else, it's the absolute bane of my existence," she said bitterly.

"And which one would that be, Mother, there tend to be so many," combatted Mom.

"It's that conniving bastard that keeps vying for my daughter's attention even though he knows full well that she's now happily engaged to a far superior man." She took one last look in the mirror and then grabbed her purse, "And if that's not enough to answer your question, he also happens to be the same one I'd blissfully castrate if ever given the chance."

"Mom, you have to stop mentioning mutilation and Jack in the same sentence," said Aunt Christine. "Someone may overhear you and think you're serious."

"Oh, but I am, dear," she answered calmly.

"Well, at least she's no longer considering scaphism," said Mom standing to leave. "I suppose that's progress."

As the four of us went downstairs to the lobby, we could see that Dad, Grandpa Anthony, Ezra, and Beau were already waiting outside by the limousine.

"You look absolutely beautiful," said Dad, kissing Mom on the cheek.

"Well, you don't look so bad yourself," she smiled.

"Oh my gosh, Mom, you have to see this," said Beau excitedly as he jumped into the back of the limo, "The lights inside this thing change color and there's even a mini disco ball!"

Mom climbed in after him. "Oh wow, this is really nice."

"Grandma, you need to see this," he said popping his head out the door. "There's two huge leather couches on both sides of the car!"

"And a chilled bottle of champagne!" called out Mom.

"Ooh, champagne!" squealed Grandma Helen, clapping her hands. "Okay, move over, darling, I'm coming in."

He quickly stepped aside and looked over at the rest of us, "Yeah, I'm thinking next time I'll just lead with the champagne."

Once the rest of us were inside, Ezra immediately leaned back and stretched out his long legs, "Okay, now this is the way road transportation was meant to be," he said. "I mean, I could literally be lying down right now and there would still be more than enough room for all of you."

"Yes, well, let's not test that theory, dear," said Grandma Helen. "I rather prefer things the way they are right now."

"You know, Dad," said Beau, gently rubbing the plush leather seat beside him, "You and Mom might really want to think about investing in one of these once we get back home."

"Oh, you do, do you?" said Dad.

"Definitely," he nodded. He pointed up at the small disco ball, "I mean, this thing alone sells it for me, what about you?"

"Yes, son, because nothing says practicability like a $300,000 limousine, with a tiny disco ball," drawled Dad. "I'll be sure to place the order just as soon as I can cash out my 401k and your mother's and my retirement savings."

"Hey, thanks Dad," he smiled. "You're good people, I don't care what Mom says."

Thirty minutes later, we found ourselves at the restaurant congregating around a long rectangular table in a private dining room offering a floor-to-ceiling view of the entire city of Positano; the stunning orange, red, and yellow hues of the setting sun complimenting the colorful cliffside town perfectly. I tried taking a few pictures, but they weren't doing it any justice, so I just stood there staring at it, searing it into my mind, so that I would never forget the beauty of this place.

As I stood there, Mom quietly came up to me and handed me a glass of wine.

"Are you sad that it's almost over?" she asked.

"A little bit, yeah," I smiled wanly. "I really love it here."

"Me too," she said. "You know, your Dad and I are hoping to start traveling more once your brother graduates."

"You and Dad have sacrificed so much for us," I said. "I hope you know that I'm grateful."

"It's what parents do," she shrugged. "I'm thankful for the time I've had with all three of you, and I'm truly proud of the people you're becoming."

"Even Beau?" I raised my brow.

"Well, the jury's still out on that one," she winked.

She slowly sipped her wine and then put her arm around me, "Listen, you're going to be starting college soon, and before you know it, you'll be out in the real world with real responsibilities. I want you to promise me that you'll take time to enjoy the parts of life that make you happy. Your Father and I chose to homeschool you because we felt that was the best decision for our family, and I don't regret it one bit, but I want you to live your life to the absolute fullest, Addie, and accomplish as much as you possibly can. The one thing I wish I'd done was travel more, but that wasn't in the cards for me, so I really encourage you to take the time to do that, if you can."

"Thanks, Mom," I said hugging her, "I love you so much."

"I love you more, baby," she smiled. "Now, let's get back to the party, shall we?"

"That sounds good," I smiled.

"Buonasera!" said a big booming voice from the doorway behind us. "My name is Arturo and I am so happy to have all of you join us this evening. As you know, Jack is a good friend of mine, and he has asked me to roll out the red carpet for all of you, so please make yourselves at home."

"Hi, Arturo, I'm Christine, thank you so much for hosting us this evening," she smiled.

He gently took her hand in his and lightly kissed it, "Jack was right, you are beyond stunning."

"Oh, uh, thank you," said Aunt Christine blushing. "That was very kind of him to say."

He then turned his attention toward Grandma Helen, "I can see exactly where you get your beauty from, your mother is simply exquisite."

"Well, aren't you adorable, dear," cooed Grandma Helen. "You know, for once I think Jack may have actually gotten something right."

"I hope you don't mind, but I took the liberty of creating a special menu for you tonight and have also brought a few bottles of wine from my own personal cellar," he smiled. "Aldo, your server, will be bringing those bottles in shortly, but for now, please continue to enjoy yourselves and I will be back to check in with you later."

As soon as Arturo made his exit, we took our seats and began reflecting on our time in Italy.

"I'd like to make a toast," said Dad, raising his glass. "I just want to take a moment to let you know that the last two weeks have been an absolute dream for me. I've had the most amazing time with each one of you and truly hope that we can all do something like this again very soon. Anthony, Helen, thank you so much for including us in this adventure of a lifetime, you have no idea how grateful we are to have been able to experience it with you."

"Thank you so much for that, dear," said Grandma Helen. "Now, I too would like to make a toast." She stood from the table and then lifted her glass, "First and foremost, I would like to thank our two beautiful daughters for joining us, you've made this vacation so much fun and I can honestly say that I've had the time of my life experiencing Italy with you, I love you both very much!"

"Aw, we love you too, Mom," they smiled.

"I'd also like to thank my wonderful son-in-law and beautiful grandchildren for coming along on this journey as well. The entire trip wouldn't have been the same without you, and I truly hope that we'll all be able to do this again very soon."

"As do we," said Dad.

"Geez, how much more is there?" mumbled Beau. "I'm tired of holding my glass up."

"You will hold it and you will smile," said Mom through gritted teeth.

Grandma Helen then turned toward Grandpa Anthony, "Anthony, you are the best time I've ever had and I am so unbelievably thankful to be able to spend the rest of my days by your side. God could not have chosen a better partner for me; you are truly the love of my life; thank you for loving me more than I deserve."

"Aw," said Mom, tears brimming in her eyes. "That's so sweet."

"Seriously, how much longer do we have to do this?" sighed Beau.

"Ti amo," said Grandpa Anthony.

"Anch'io ti amo," she smiled, bending down to kiss him.

"Can we please finish this, I'm actually thirsty now," said Beau.

She raised her glass high into the air and then stopped abruptly, a look of anger distorting her face, "You bastard, I knew you were going to show up!"

Completely caught off guard by her verbal assault, we immediately turned around to see who she was talking to.

"Hello, everyone," waved Jack timidly. "Nice to see you, Helen."

"Oh my God, Jack, what are you doing here?" asked Aunt Christine.

"Well, I hope you don't mind my stopping by, but I was here on business and thought I'd swing in and say hello," he said. "I hope Arturo's taking good care of you."

"Just stopping by, are you?" said Grandma Helen. "Then why are you carrying that large bouquet of roses?"

"Well, I didn't want to come empty-handed, so I thought I'd bring these for Chris," he said, handing her the bouquet.

"Her name is Christine, not Chris," spat Grandma Helen. "I can't stand it when you call her that."

"Apologies, Helen," he said. "I meant no disrespect."

"A little late for that, don't you think?" she snarled.

"You know, Jack, this may not be the best time," said Grandpa Anthony. "We're here to celebrate our last night together and should probably get back to that if you don't mind."

"I apologize for the disturbance, Anthony, but I really need to talk to Christine for a moment." He turned toward her, "Could I maybe speak with you in private?"

"You son of a bitch!" yelled Grandma Helen, grabbing a fork off the table. "I knew you were up to no good, I just knew it!"

"Please put the fork down, Mother," said Mom quietly. "We've made it this far without you being thrown into an Italian prison and I'd really like for that to continue."

"Mother, please, I'll handle this," said Aunt Christine. "But, my Dad's right, this really isn't a good time, Jack."

"It will only take a minute, I promise," he said. "We can talk right outside the door, so you won't be far from your family."

"Okay fine," she sighed. "But I'm serious, this needs to be short."

She set the flowers down on the table and followed him out the door.

"I swear, if he does one thing to upset her or tries to weasel his way back into her life, I'm going to cut off his balls," growled Grandma Helen. "Italian prison be damned."

"Holy crap, forget unleashing the hounds, I say we just unleash Grandma," said Beau proudly.

"Dude, I know," said Ezra. "Remind me never to cross her, I'd really like for my manhood to stay intact."

We stood there staring awkwardly at each other for a few minutes and then finally made a beeline to the door where Grandma Helen was listening. Although the words were somewhat muffled, we were still able to make out parts of the conversation as we all leaned in as close as we could to the door's opening without being seen.

"Okay, you have me here," said Aunt Christine. "What is it that you need to say?"

"You know, I honestly saw this going differently in my head," he laughed.

"Well, whatever it is, just say it," she answered coolly.

"Okay, but I really need you to just let me finish everything I have to say before you say anything, alright?" he said.

"Fine," she agreed.

"Look, I'm not going to lie, I miss you, Christine," he said. "I have felt so lost ever since our divorce and I absolutely hate myself for hurting you the way that I did. You were the best thing to ever happen to me and I completely blew it, I know that now. I was incredibly immature while we were married, and I definitely made a lot of mistakes, but I'm a different man now, and I am willing to do whatever it takes to get you to give me another chance. I know that I was selfish, inconsiderate, and one hundred percent in the wrong, but I also know that we had something really special, and I want to get that back."

"I'm going to kill him!" hissed Grandma Helen, launching toward the door.

"No, you're not," said Mom, holding her back. "You're going to let Chrissy handle this, she's stronger than you know."

"And I realize that this comes at a very inopportune time, considering your recent engagement," he continued, "but I thought we might try spending another week here figuring things out together and maybe rekindle that spark we once had. I still love you, Chris, and I know that I can make you happy, I just need you to give me the chance to do that."

The silence that filled the room was almost deafening as we waited for her response.

"Chris, I literally just poured my heart out to you, do you seriously have nothing to say?"

"Oh, I'm sorry, are you done?" she asked aloofly. "Because if you are, I'd have to say that's the biggest load of shit I've ever heard, and I've heard plenty, believe me."

"Hey now, wait a minute—" he started to say.

"No, you wait a minute!" she seethed. "I listened to what you had to say and now you are going to listen to me."

"Oh, this is going to hurt," whispered Ezra.

"She's about to verbally spank him so hard!" said Beau. "Dang, I wish I had some popcorn."

"Shh!" said Mom. "Stop talking, I want to hear this."

"For you to stand here and tell me that we were so good together and that you still love me is disgusting. Our marriage was a complete joke, Jack, and you more than anyone should know that. You lied, cheated, and then had the audacity to make me think that it was my fault because I wasn't good enough for you, that I didn't measure up to your standards, and now that I'm happily moving on with my life, you're seriously going to stand here and ask me for another chance, how dare you! You literally slept with my best friend, and God knows how many other people, and expect me to give it another try?"

"Oh, man, he's dying out there!" said Beau.

"No shit, Abe Lincoln had a better future after picking up his tickets from the box office," laughed Ezra.

"Listen, Jack, I'm getting ready to marry the man of my dreams, a man you could never even hold a candle to, so please just do us all a favor and stay out the hell out of my life; I don't have the energy, nor the desire, to put up with your bullshit anymore."

"Christine, I know you don't mean that," he said.

"I mean every single word, Jack, I really do," she said. "I want you completely out of my life. Not only have you ruined the last night of my vacation with my family, but now I'm going to have to go back in there and apologize to my Mother because she is the only one who saw through your lies. She kept warning me that you were up to no good and I stupidly continued to defend you, but no more, I'm done."

"Chris, please don't do this," he implored. "We can get past this; I know we can."

"You know what, even if I was remotely interested in getting back together with you, this whole guise of friendship you tried to pull off is causing me to have to go back in there and watch my Mother gloat, and that, as you well know, is completely unforgivable, so thanks a lot, asshole!"

Upon hearing those last words from Aunt Christine, Grandma Helen perked up and smiled haughtily, "See, I told you he was up to something."

CHAPTER TWENTY-FOUR

"I feel so stupid," said Aunt Christine. "How could I have not seen it?"

"You're not stupid," I said. "You couldn't have possibly known what he was planning on doing."

"Yes, I am," she said. "I was too stupid to see through him, and I hate myself for it. I mean, I actually believed that he wanted to be friends, that he was truly happy for me and Brian."

"You can't keep beating yourself up over this, Chrissy," said Mom. "There was no way for you to know what he was up to; he surprised all of us when he showed up, none of us were expecting it."

"Ahem," said Grandma Helen, dramatically clearing her throat. "I wouldn't say that's entirely true, dear, some of us were actually paying attention to the signs, but then again, I digress."

We were sitting in the hotel lobby waiting for the shuttle to drive us back to the train station in Naples. All of the ferries that day had been canceled (don't ask me why, the weather was absolutely beautiful), so we had to make other arrangements. The guys were waiting outside, but Mom, Grandma Helen, and I decided to wait inside with Aunt Christine, who was still upset over what had happened last night.

"Okay, you just thought he was up to something," said Mom. "You had absolutely no idea that he was going to show up unannounced like he did, and you know it."

"The point is I tried to warn you," she said. "The man is a contemptible ass; he always has been and he always will be, that alone should have been enough to tell you that he's not to be trusted."

"Yes, Mother, you made that abundantly clear last night," said Aunt Christine. "And again, I apologize for not believing you, but I think you've made your point."

"Would you please excuse us?" said Mom, pulling Grandma Helen aside. "I just need a moment with Mom."

They walked over and stood behind a tall ficus tree, "Okay, listen, you've had plenty of time to gloat, but now it's time to stop," said Mom. "You spent the entire evening last night making sure that everyone knew you were right, but enough is enough, so just knock it off, okay?"

"But-" she started to say.

"No buts, Mother," said Mom, shaking her head. "You're not helping Christine by continuing to rub salt in her wound, she's upset enough as it is and she doesn't need you reveling in the fact that you were right and she was wrong."

"But I was right," she said indignantly. "In fact, I was the only one to see through his spurious act, and I think that deserves a little more recognition."

"You have received plenty of recognition already," said Mom. "And you're only making things worse by continuing to brag, so just stop."

"I am not bragging, I'm simply telling everyone that I was right…which I was," she said petulantly.

"Mother, would you please just stop and listen to what I'm saying?"

"Okay, fine, I'm listening," she said aloofly.

"No, you're not, you're mentally reloading," said Mom.

"Well, what am I supposed to do when she allowed him to weasel his way back into her life so easily?" she said. "That man is an arrogant bastard and the fact that he showed up last night thinking that he could just whisk her away is proof of what I'm saying. Now, I'm sorry if I seem unsympathetic, but that man is an absolute cad and has no business being in her life, end of story."

"I'm pretty sure they both figured that out yesterday, Mom," she smiled wanly.

"Yes, but I don't want it to happen again," she sighed. "I can't stand seeing her get hurt by someone who doesn't even deserve to breathe the same air she does, she's always been too good for him and I need her to see that."

"She does see that, and last night was proof of it," said Mom. "Christine didn't waver once, and Jack was left looking like the fool he is, it's actually somewhat comical if you think about it."

"He did look rather pained to see that she wasn't interested in his proposal," she grinned. "The tortured expression on his face alone made the night almost worth it."

"Look, I know you love her very much," said Mom. "But you have to trust that she's learned her lesson and that she's smart enough to keep him out of her life permanently. Put your ego aside and stop making her feel bad for not listening to you, it's only going to cause her more stress."

"I suppose you're right, darling," she sighed.

"And if he does ever try to weasel his way back into her good graces, you have my full permission to neuter him right on the spot," said Mom. "In fact, I'll even hold him down while you do it."

"Well, now I'm kind of hoping he does make another appearance," she drawled. "And if he does, just know that I'll happily take the blame, there's really no sense in the two of us having to sit behind bars."

"I love you so much," chuckled Mom.

I love you too, darling," she smiled. She turned to leave and then quickly called over her shoulder, "But I meant what I said, his balls are mine the minute he steps anywhere near her."

The shuttle finally arrived and our driver, Roberto, who was the most adorable-looking man, helped us with our luggage and then happily chatted with us as he drove us out of the city of Positano.

"So much traffic," said Roberto.

"Is it normally this bad?" asked Dad.

"Well, since we are coming into peak season, yes," he said. "It's because of all the tourists and their rented scooters and cars, they don't know how to drive these streets and are very dangerous to those of us who do."

"I can imagine," said Grandpa Anthony. "These roads can be quite treacherous."

"See, over there, tourist!" said Roberto pointing at an oncoming sedan. "You can see how scared he looks all scrunched up over the steering wheel, he has no clue what to do, he's like a baby."

"Oh my gosh, this guy's hilarious," laughed Ezra.

"Ah, see, two more rentals over there," said Roberto smugly. "More tourists, more cars, more mess."

"I had no idea so many people rented vehicles here," said Dad. "I wouldn't think it really necessary with all the buses, ferries, and taxis."

"Ah, that is because you are a smart man!" he said, quickly turning the wheel to avoid hitting an oncoming car, "Ugh, see, there's another one."

"Well, I see that lanes are simply a suggestion here," said Beau, playing a game on his phone. "You should fit right in, Addie, considering what a terrible driver you are."

"Shut up, Beau," I snapped.

"Oh my God, we're going to die," said Mom.

"No, you won't die," smiled Roberto, looking in the rearview mirror. "If anyone dies, it will be the rental people; I do this all the time, you're perfectly safe."

As we made our way up the steep and narrow winding road, we eventually came upon a long line of traffic, which then caused Roberto to scream and shout as he flailed his arms about wildly.

"Non ci credo, che idiota fa questo?" he yelled angrily, honking his horn. "Spostalo! Spostalo!"

"Gee, something tells me that Roberto is displeased," snarked Beau. "I can't imagine what it could possibly be."

"Roberto, darling, I do hope this doesn't end up taking too long," said Grandma Helen. "I don't want to miss our train; I have absolutely no desire to be in Naples any longer than I have to be. You must get us through this traffic."

"Oh, this will clear up in no time," answered Roberto. "It's probably just a-"

"Tourist?" said Beau finishing his sentence.

"Molto bene, you're learning!" he said excitedly.

It took us about ten minutes, but we eventually moved up far enough to see what had been holding up the traffic. A young man and woman were standing on the side of the road yelling at each other angrily while a red and black scooter lay on the ground behind them. It didn't look as though either one was hurt, but they were definitely not happy and were obviously blaming each other for what had happened.

"Ugh, tourists," hissed Roberto irritably. "I'm so sick and tired of tourists."

We were able to arrive at the train station with plenty of time to spare, so we quickly grabbed some lunch before boarding the train that would eventually take us back to Rome. From there it would be another quick train ride to the Leonardo da Vinci Fiumicino Airport, where we would catch the flight home back to Atlanta.

After making our way through security, we still had about thirty minutes before boarding, so we found a few scattered seats close to the gate and waited for our flight to be called.

"Well, this trip has been nothing short of eventful, especially after last night," said Grandma Helen. "I wonder what poor Jack is up to right now, the son of a bitch."

"I don't know and I don't care," grumbled Aunt Christine. "I just want to put yesterday behind me."

"Christine, darling," she said, putting an arm around her. "I don't think I've told you how proud I am of how you handled that whole thing with Jack last night. You were so calm and composed, whereas I would have probably slapped him across the face just to hear the sound it would make."

"Believe me, it crossed my mind a few times," she chuckled. "But I didn't want to give him the satisfaction of thinking he'd hurt me, which he didn't. I just hate that I believed him when he said that he just wanted to be friends, I feel like such a fool."

"You're not a fool, dear, just a tad bit too trusting, that's all," she said.

"Yeah, well, I suppose if I'd just listened to you I wouldn't have had to deal with any of it," she sighed. "You were right all along and I was just too blind to see it, I'm really sorry, Mom."

"Thank you, darling, I appreciate you saying that," she smiled. "But you don't have to apologize to me."

"Wait, I'm sorry, what did you just say?" asked Aunt Christine confusedly. "I don't think I heard that correctly."

"I said you don't owe me an apology, dear," she said again. "It's all over and done with, so let's just move past it and get on with our lives."

"So, wait, you have no intention of prattling on and on about all the times you tried to warn me or point out my every mistake in great detail?"

"Nope," she chirped quietly.

"And you're actually going to let this whole thing go and not rub my nose in any of it?"

"Uh-huh, yes," nodded Grandma Helen noncommittally. "That would be correct."

"I'm sorry, I don't buy it," she said. "You've never been one to let anything go, so obviously there's something else happening here, what is it?"

"Okay fine," she relented irritably. "Your sister has forbidden me to gloat anymore, so now I have to bite my tongue and keep quiet."

"Oh my God, that must be pure torture for you," laughed Aunt Christine.

"Well, it's certainly not been easy, but I am trying," she sighed.

"I love you, Mom, I hope you know that," she smiled. "I know that you were only trying to protect me and I'm so sorry I didn't listen to you. I think I just wanted to salvage a friendship with someone that was once very special to me, and maybe show him that he didn't break me, that I'm actually much happier without him than I ever was with him. I know that may seem silly, but it's true."

"I love you too, dear," said Grandma Helen. "You confidently stood your ground and showed him that you were completely over him, I honestly don't think he saw any of that coming."

"Yeah, well, pompous asses rarely do," she said. "I will say the look on his face while I rebuked him was priceless, I only wish I'd had a camera to capture it."

"No need to worry about that, darling," smiled Grandma Helen, pulling out her phone. "I have more than plenty and I'm happy to share."

"Oh, my God, you didn't!" she gasped.

"Oh, but I did," she nodded. "And many of them are close-ups."

"Mother, I could kiss you right now," exclaimed Aunt Christine. "You have to let me see them!"

Grandma Helen proudly handed over her phone, "You know, I was thinking I might even put them up on my Facebook-"

"Absolutely not, Mother," she shook her head emphatically. "I don't need my personal life splattered all over your Facebook feed."

"Okay, fine," she pouted. "I guess I'll just have to make a few copies and be sure to send him one, you know, as a token of my loathing."

Just then a young mother and her screaming toddler made their way over to our gate and took a seat opposite us.

"Waa! Waa! Waa!"

Oh dear God, please tell me that thing is not on our flight," said Grandma Helen.

It's not a thing, Mother, it's a child," said Aunt Christine.

"Waa! Waa! Waa!"

The mother handed him a toy robot and he immediately threw it on the ground, "I no want it!"

"Caleb, honey, please quiet down and play with Mr. Robot," she pleaded with him.

"No!" he snapped.

"Caleb, please, try to stay calm," she said. "Mommy has a headache."

"Waa! Waa! Waa!"

The wailing continued incessantly for another few minutes until Caleb bolted out of his stroller and began flapping his arms up and down while screaming and running around in circles.

"Caleb, no," said the mother, trying to limit his movement. "You're not a pterodactyl, remember?"

"Yes I am!" he screamed.

"No, Caleb, pterodactyls don't act like this in airports," she said. "They wait until they're outside to play."

"You know, I'm thinking I may have to just kill Caleb," said Grandma Helen, rubbing her temples. "My nerves simply can't handle him right now and the thought of having to spend the next ten hours listening to his piercing screams is more than I can bear."

"Grandma, he's just a boy," I said. "I'm sure he'll eventually calm down."

"Oh my God, I'm going to kill that child," hissed Mom taking a seat next to us. "Can she not get him under control?"

"Maybe we can slip him a Benadryl when she's not looking," said Grandma Helen rifling through her purse. "I think I still may have a few."

"Mother, you cannot drug that child!" said Aunt Christine.

"You want to make a bet?" she said.

"Caleb, no, you're not a pterodactyl!" said the mother repeatedly as she chased after him. "You need to stop this right now!"

"No!" he yelled. "I no stop!"

As Caleb continued to ignore his mother and scream bloody murder, a soft voice came over the loudspeaker announcing our flight, "Good evening, we will now begin boarding flight 7568 to Atlanta, Georgia.

Please be sure to have your passports and boarding pass ready as this will make the process much smoother for everyone."

"Excuse me," said the frazzled Mother. "Did she just say that this plane is going to Atlanta?"

"Yes," I nodded.

She looked down at her boarding pass, "Oh no, Caleb, we're at the wrong gate!"

"Uh oh," he sang out happily.

"We're actually over there," she said, pointing across the way.

"Okay, I fly!" he giggled. "Just like terdaktal."

"Okay, you fly and Mommy will follow," she said. "Fly fast, Caleb, I'm right behind you!"

"Oh, thank God, he's gone," said Grandma Helen. "It's a good thing too because I'm actually all out of Benadryl and only have this one Ambien, although I suppose I could have just cut it in half, that probably would have worked equally as well."

"Please tell me she's joking," whispered Aunt Christine uneasily. "She wouldn't really do something like that, right?"

"Chrissy, the woman used to regularly drug us with Benadryl anytime we spent more than three hours in a car," said Mom. "What do you think?"

CHAPTER TWENTY-FIVE

"Oh, just stop it, you're being absolutely ridiculous," scoffed Mom. "And the fake vomiting sounds need to go, you're folding laundry, not cleaning up roadkill."

"Mom, this is so gross," said Beau, holding up Dad's underwear. "It may as well be roadkill."

Well, you should have thought about that before dumping the entire contents of your suitcase on top of our delicates," said Mom. "Now you get to help me fold everything."

It had been a few days since we returned home from Italy and everyone was doing their best to get back into the groove of things. Dad and Ezra were back at work, Grandma Helen started rehearsals for her next production, Grandpa Anthony was riding his Harley, Aunt Christine was planning her wedding, Beau and I were preparing to enjoy a summer off from school, and Mom was currently trying to get the house back in order.

"You told me to unpack and I did," said Beau. "I don't understand why you're so upset."

"Unpack, yes, not jettison your clothes directly out of your luggage and into the washer," she said, pointing to his suitcase sitting in the corner. "Seriously, Beau, did you ever stop to think that you may still have some clean clothes in there, that maybe you should take a few minutes to sort through what you had so that you wouldn't have to wash everything?"

"Okay, I think you and I both know the answer to that question," he drawled sarcastically.

"You know what, never mind," she sighed. "This is almost done, so why don't you just go and get that big bag of dog food out of the trunk, and we'll call it even, okay?"

"Yes ma'am," he said exasperatedly. "Is the car unlocked or do I need to get the keys?"

"It should still be unlocked, but you may want to take them just in case," she said.

Mom quickly finished folding the laundry and then walked into the kitchen where Aunt Christine and I were looking at bridal magazines.

"Anything catching your eye?" she asked.

"No, not really," said Aunt Christine. "I'm honestly just trying to get some ideas right now, although there are a few good articles discussing venues and color themes."

"And what kind of venue do you think you and Brian will want?" she asked.

"I'm not quite sure," she said. "We really don't want to have a large wedding, but then again, we don't want anything too small either. We're really just trying to figure everything out, so it's all still up in the air."

"Well, whatever you do, I would suggest keeping it under wraps and away from Mom because she's already started her guest list and it is anything but small," said Mom. "She's added names of people that none of us have spoken to in years."

"Ugh, of course she has," sighed Aunt Christine. "This is going to be my second marriage, surely none of those people even care if they get an invite."

Yeah, well, I still think you should play it close to the vest," said Mom. That way if you decide to go small, she'll have no other option than to whittle it down, and her arguments will be futile."

"You know, that actually makes a lot of sense," she said. "Make it so that she has no other choice than to work with what she's given, that should help alleviate quite a bit of stress."

"Okay, so I've got the food," said Beau, holding a large bag of dog food. "Where do you want me to put it?"

"Why don't you go ahead and put it in the garage and I'll fill the container later," said Mom.

"You do realize I'm just going to be cleaning all of this up over the next month, right?" he snarked.

"Oh, It'll be good for you and it'll give you something fun to do over the summer," she smiled.

"That's not funny, Mom," he grunted. "Ezra and Addie don't have to clean up after Churchill, it's only me."

"Well, you can always take over cleaning the bathrooms for Addie," she offered.

"Is that my only choice?" he asked.

"Pretty much, yes," she nodded.

"I can't say that I find either of those options very appealing," he said. "In fact, I find them both equally disgusting."

"Well, it would seem that you're standing at a bit of a crossroads and have a decision to make, yes?" she said.

"What difference does it make, either way, I'm in hell," he grumbled, taking the food into the garage. "Oh, and if it's alright with you, I'm going to head over to Tyler's after this, his mom made homemade cinnamon rolls and saved a few for me; she says they're better than the canned ones you make."

"Okay, honey, that's fine," she said.

"Tyler's Mom sounds like a piece of work," said Aunt Christine.

"Ugh, she's one of those fake nice people who always make condescending comments about anyone who doesn't shop at a farmers market," snarled Mom. "I can't stand her."

"Hey, you aren't seriously going to make me exchange chores with Beau are you?" I asked. "I really don't want to have to clean up after Churchill."

"Oh, don't worry about him, he just likes to complain," she said dismissively. "You and I both know the bathrooms will present way too much work, and the minute he realizes that, he's going to pick up his little poop shovel and be on his merry little way; your brother is nothing if not predictable."

"Darling have our cases of wine come in yet?" asked Grandma Helen walking through the back door. "I'm craving that delicious chianti we had at that charming little winery and think it will be the perfect early afternoon pick-me-up."

"Isn't that why most people drink coffee?" I asked.

"Your Grandmother's not most people, honey," said Mom. "Coffee is strictly a morning drink in her world."

"We barely ordered it a week ago, Mom, it's going to take some time to get here," said Aunt Christine.

"Well, now I'm even more depressed," she said, taking a seat next to me.

"Why, what's wrong," asked Mom.

"Well, I think I'm just really missing Italy," she sighed. "It's just not the same here, you know?"

"Yeah, I'm pretty depressed too, Grandma," I said commiseratively.

"I think we all are," said Mom. "That's the worst part about going on vacation. You inevitably have to come back to reality and be reminded of how boring and monotonous your life really is; it's no wonder we're all depressed."

"Actually, dear, I think that may only be you," said Grandma Helen. "My life is absolutely fabulous, it's just that I think I'd rather be doing it in Italy, that's all."

"Gee, thanks, Mom," she said. "You really know how to make someone feel good about themselves."

Grandma Helen looked over at the stack of magazines that were sitting on the counter and picked one up, "Ooh, wedding magazines, are we finally entering into the planning phase?"

"I'm just getting some ideas, Mother, nothing more," said Aunt Christine.

"Well, have you at least set a date?" she asked. "You know, I was thinking a fall wedding would be perfect, especially with the leaves changing and everything."

"It's already May, Mom, there's no way for me to plan a wedding in that short of time," she said.

"What about winter wedding, then?" she pressed. "We could have a winter wonderland theme and you could wear a tiara just like Cinderella, you would look absolutely stunning, Christine."

"You can't possibly be serious," she rolled her eyes. "I am not wearing a tiara, Mother, you know me better than that."

"Well, can we at least go and try on wedding dresses?" she asked petulantly. "I want to drink champagne and preen over my beautiful daughter as she tries on multiple gowns."

"Oh please, Mother, you just want everyone to know you're the mother of the bride," said Mom. "It has very little to do with Christine and you know it."

"Okay, fine, but the champagne part was true," she capitulated. "It's always so much fun to have them wait on you hand and foot and treat you like you're a celebrity; this may be the last time I get to experience it unless we can get Addie married off soon."

"Oh my gosh, Grandma, are you serious?" I asked.

"Not entirely, dear, no," she said. "But it might be fun to go and pretend a few times don't you think?"

"Mother, you are not taking my eighteen-year-old daughter to try on wedding dresses," said Mom. "That's absurd."

"Party pooper," she grumbled.

"Okay, Mom, I'm headed to off work, I'll see you tonight," said Ezra walking into the kitchen.

"Oh, already?" she said looking at the clock. "Have you eaten anything; do you need me to make you something?"

"No, I'm just going to grab something at Mojangs," he said. "I'm kind of craving one of their chicken biscuits."

"Oh my God, Ezra, for the last time, please stop calling it Mojangs, it's Bojangles," she closed her eyes in frustration. "I really hate when you deliberately mispronounce words."

"I know, that's why I do it," he smiled devilishly. He grabbed his keys and headed out the back door, "Okay, well, I love y'all!"

"We love you too, honey," said Mom. "Please be safe and call me if you need me."

As soon as he left, Grandma Helen clapped her hands together and said, "You know, all of this wedding talk has me in such a festive mood, what do you say we open a bottle of wine and chat about wedding ideas."

"Like I said, Mom, I'm not ready to commit to anything, so if you can promise me that you're not going to push things onto me like you normally do, then that sounds good to me."

"Christine, darling, I wouldn't dream of ever doing something so dastardly," she said. "This is your wedding and I promise to do my absolute best to abide by your wishes. Of course, if you decide to get married in Tuscany, you're going to need to let me know, especially now that your father and I are looking at property over there."

"Wait, what?" exclaimed Aunt Christine.

"Oh, my God, Mom, are you serious?" asked Mom.

"Grandma, that would be so cool!" I said.

"So you and Dad are actually thinking about moving to Italy?" said Mom.

"Not moving, no," she shook her head. "We're just thinking about buying a vacation home. Your father really enjoyed reconnecting with his roots and I absolutely love it there, so we just thought we might look into buying a house; that way everyone can use it and it would serve as a nice escape for your father and me."

"Well, now that is definitely something to celebrate," said Mom. "I'll get the wine!"

"So, when do you think this is going to happen?" I asked.

"We honestly don't know, dear, but I'm hoping sometime within the next year," she said. "That's why I mentioned having the wedding over there, it would be the perfect place to get married don't you think?"

"Oh, I don't know, Mom," said Aunt Christine. "I'd really have to talk with Brian, plus there are a ton of other variables that would need to be taken into consideration before I could ever agree to do something so extravagant."

"And that's why I mentioned it, darling," she smiled. "It's simply an option, that's all."

"Well, this is definitely cause for celebration," said Mom. "I've been saving this bottle of cabernet for a special occasion and I think that this is the perfect time to open it."

"I'm so excited for you and Dad," said Aunt Christine. "This is going to open a whole new chapter in your lives, it's like a dream come true."

Mom handed each of us a glass and then raised her own, "To exciting new beginnings, may they bring peace, joy, and happiness to us all, salute!"

"Salute!" we shouted.

"So Mom, tell me, will this be a place that you and Dad will be frequenting often?" asked Mom. "You know, maybe spend a few months out of every year?"

"And give up the theater, never," she shook her head. "I have found my calling, darling, and my fans need me here, so no, it will strictly be a vacation home." She peered coyly over the rim of her wine glass, "Besides, I'm the one that keeps things exciting around here, whatever would you do without me?"

"You mean besides saving what's left of my sanity and liver?" said Mom, "You know, I honestly haven't a clue."

"As much as you hate to admit it, dear, you know you need me," she said with a self-satisfying grin. "Now, let's crack open another bottle and start planning this wedding!"

The End.

A Letter From Tiffany

Thank you so much for reading *"Traveled and Unraveled: A Delightfully Dysfunctional Familial Vacation,"* the third installment in the Delightfully Dysfunctional series. I hope you had as much fun reading it as I had writing it. My husband and I took the very same vacation that the Jenkins did, which is what initially inspired me to write this book. If you haven't already, please be sure to check out the first two books in the series, *"Crazed and Confused"* and *"Jingled and Jangled."* The Jenkins are very near and dear to my heart, so you can rest assured that I have quite a few more books planned for the series, with the fourth installment heading your way in 2025.

I always love hearing from my readers, so please feel free to drop me a message anytime via Facebook, Instagram, and/or my personal website. My interaction with you is what motivates me to write, so please reach out anytime. Facebook and Instagram are where I share information on new and upcoming books, major announcements, book signings, etc., so please be sure to follow me there so that you can stay informed and up to date on things.

Facebook Page: https://www.facebook.com/TiffanyRyanAuthor

Instagram Page: https://www.instagram.com/tiffany_ryan_author

Website: tiffanyryanwrites.com

Sincerely,
Tiffany

ACKNOWLEDGEMENTS

I've said this more than once, but it takes a group of talented and selfless individuals to help just about any Indy author publish a book. Thankfully, God has placed a few amazing individuals in my corner, and for that, I will be eternally grateful.

First and foremost, I would like to thank Tambi Smith, who has selflessly given so much of her time and talent to help me bring the Jenkins to life. She is my sounding board, personal cheerleader, editor, and has become one of my very best friends. She keeps me sane when I think I'm losing my mind and constantly motivates me to stay on track. Thank you for being my rock, Tambi, your friendship means the world to me.

I would also like to thank my mother, Kathleen Catalano, for being my greatest cheerleader and biggest supporter. Your willingness to tell everyone and their mother about me and my books is probably what keeps me in business, thank you for always having my back.

Gabriel and McKenna, there would be no Jenkins family if it weren't for you, thank you for the endless material you provide me daily. I suppose I owe you both royalties, but for now, my love will have to suffice.

Lastly, I would like to thank my husband, Blake, for always having faith in me, even when I didn't have faith in myself. You are the best travel partner any girl could ask for, here's to many more adventures with you by my side.